Tiger lily

Also by
JODI LYNN ANDERSON

Peaches
The Secrets of Peaches
Love and Peaches

JODI LYNN ANDERSON

Tiger lily

HARPER TEEN
An Imprint of HarperCollinsPublishers

HarperTeen is an imprint of HarperCollins Publishers.

Tiger Lily

Library of Congress Cataloging-in-Publication Data
Anderson, Jodi Lynn.
    Tiger Lily / Jodi Lynn Anderson — 1st ed.
        p.   cm.
    Summary: Fifteen-year-old Tiger Lily receives special protections
from the spiritual forces of Neverland, but then she meets her tribe's most
dangerous enemy—Peter Pan—and falls in love with him.
    ISBN 978-0-06-200325-6
    [1. Fairies—Fiction.   2. Love—Fiction.   3. Magic—Fiction.]   I. Barrie,
J. M. (James Matthew),   1860–1937. Peter Pan.   II. Title.
PZ7.A53675Ti 2012   2011032659
[Fic]—dc23   CIP
                                                                              AC

Typography by Erin Fitzsimmons
12 13 14 15 16 CG/RRDH 10 9 8 7 6 5 4 3 2 1
❖
First Edition

For the girls with messy hair and thirsty hearts

I am not to speak to you, I am to think of you when I sit alone or wake at night alone,

I am to wait, I do not doubt I am to meet you again,

I am to see to it that I do not lose you.

—Walt Whitman, "To a Stranger"

Tiger lily

She stands on the cliffs, near the old crumbling stone house.

There's nothing left in the house but an upturned table, a ladle, and a clay bowl. She stands for more than an hour, goose-bumped and shivering. At these times, she won't confide in me. She runs her hands over her body, as if checking that it's still there, her heart pulsing and beating. The limbs are smooth and strong, thin and sinewy, her hair long and black and messy and gleaming despite her age. You wouldn't know it to look at her, that she's lived long enough to look for what's across the water. Eighty years later, and she is still fifteen.

These days, there is no new world. The maps have long since settled and stayed put. People know the shapes of Africa, Asia, and South America. And they know which beasts were mythical and which weren't. Manatees are real, mermaids aren't.

Rhinoceroses exist and sea monsters don't. There are no more sea serpents guarding deadly whirlpools. There are pirates, yes, but there is nothing romantic about them. The rest is all stories, and stories have been put in their place.

Now, the outsiders keep their eyes on their own shores, and we keep our eyes on ours. Too far off route, we've been overlooked, and most of us don't think about the world outside. Only she and I are different. Every month or so she comes here and stares toward the ocean, and all the village children whisper about her, even her own. It has become such a ritual.

And when she surfaces from her dream, she calls me by my old name, though no one uses it anymore. And she turns to me, her eyelashes fluttering in the glare that surrounds me, and whispers to me in one short syllable.

Tink.

ONE

L et me tell you something straight off. This is a love story, but not like any you've heard. The boy and the girl are far from innocent. Dear lives are lost. And good doesn't win. In some places, there is something ultimately good about endings. In Neverland, that is not the case.

To understand what it's like to be a faerie, tall as a walnut and genetically gifted with wings—who happened to witness such a series of events—you must first understand that all faeries are mute. Somewhere in our evolution, on our long crooked journey from amoeba to dragonfly to faerie, nature must have decided language wasn't necessary for us to survive. It's good in some ways, not to have a language. It makes you *see* things. You turn your attention, not to babbling about yourself, broadcasting each and every thought to everyone within earshot—as people often do—but to observing. That's how faeries became so empathic. We're so attuned to the beating of a heart, the varied thrum of a pulse, the zaps of the synapses of a brain, that we are almost inside others' minds. Most faeries tune this out by only spending time with other faeries. They make settlements in tree stumps and barely venture out except to hunt mosquitoes. I get bored by that. I like to fly and keep an eye on things. That was how I saw it, from the beginning. Some would like to call it being nosy. That's what my mother would say, at least.

That morning, I was on my way to see about some locusts. They'd invaded and eaten all the good parts of a faerie settlement near the river, and I had never seen a locust before. I was flying along on a curiosity mission when I passed the girls in a manioc field.

They were out cultivating the tubers—in the tribe, a woman's job. All in their early teens: some of the girls were awkwardly growing but still thoroughly in their skin, with gangly limbs that expressed their most passing thoughts, while others were curvy, and carrying those curves like new tools they were learning. I recognized Tiger Lily instantly; I had seen her before. She stood out like a combination of a roving panther and a girl. She *stalked* instead of walked. Her body still held the invincibility of a child, when at her age it should have been giving way to fragile, flexible curves.

These were Sky Eaters, a tribe whose lives were always turned toward the river. They fished, and grew manioc in the clearing along its shore. A Sky Eater wandering far into the thick, unnavigable forest was like a faerie wandering into a hawk's hunting territory. It happened only rarely. So when they heard the crashing through the trees, most of the girls screamed. Tiger Lily reached for her hatchet.

Stone came through first, splitting through the branches. The other boys rallied behind him. And Pine Sap, last and weakest of them all, brought up the rear. They were all breathless, shirtless, a muscular and well-organized group with weedy Pine Sap trailing at the back.

Stone gestured for the girls to come with them. "You'll never believe it."

The girls followed the boys through the forest, and I grabbed a tassel of Tiger Lily's tunic because I, too, was curious, and she ran faster than I wanted to fly. And then we cleared the last of the trees leading to the cliffs, and the way to the sea was open, and I heard a noise escape Tiger Lily's lips, a little cry, and heard it on the other girls' lips too as they arrived behind her. There upon the water was a large ship, a skeleton against the sky, collapsed and flailing into the rocks close to shore, broken apart and drowning. The scene was all deep blues and grays and whites and the wild waves lifting it all like deep gasping breaths.

Looking closer, I could see little pink people—tiny, falling and clinging. I knew right away they must be Englanders, a people we knew of from across the ocean.

"They're dying," one of the girls breathed—a reedy thing I knew to be named Moon Eye—gesturing with her thin arms.

Between the ship's decks, the rocks soared. Pieces of it raced into the sea and disappeared. Little people dropped from it in droves.

Pine Sap elbowed Tiger Lily's arm; he pointed, his finger snaking to trace a line farther in. One little rowboat moved toward shore like a water bug, but we could see that it was caught in the breakers.

It had only one occupant—a fragile figure, a lone man. He was making for the shore with all his might and getting nowhere. As we looked on, the waves buffeted him, until finally he was knocked from the boat, though he somehow managed to cling to its bow. He looked to be as good as dead. But seconds later, he hurled himself back on board.

The tiny boat looked fit to capsize, was half full of water already, and the man was not an adept seaman, constantly turning the boat broadwise when it should have been pointed vertically against the waves. Still, he rowed, and rowed, and despite everything, and to our utter surprise, the boat suddenly lurched its way out of the breakers and into the calm waters by the beach. He collapsed down and forward for a moment, as if he might be dead, and then began to row, calmly, toward the shore. Several people in our group let out their breaths. I did too, though no one would have heard me.

To me it seemed like he was trading one deadly place for another, and that drifting back out to sea was no less dangerous than walking into the island without knowing its dangers. The forest would eat him alive, even his bones.

The young people of the tribe were all looking at each other with a combination of exhilaration and fear, except for Tiger Lily, stony and unreadable, her eyes on the man below. Pine Sap grabbed her hand and pulled her back from the cliff's edge; she had been standing so close the wind might have blown her over.

"They'll be deciding what to do about him," Stone said.

Because all Neverlanders knew what danger Englanders brought with them.

The children raced home to see what the village council would do. I stayed and watched the ship floundering in the waves for a while longer, then flew to catch up.

That was the beginning, or at least the beginning of the beginning, of the changes that were coming for Tiger Lily: the arrival of one little man on one little lifeboat. By that day, I had known of Tiger Lily for years. I also knew a little of her history: that Tik Tok, the shaman, had found her while he was out gathering wild lettuce for medicine, under a flower—either abandoned there or hidden from some peril by someone who didn't survive to come back for her. He'd named her Tiger Lily, after the flower she was under, bundled her into his arms, and taken her home. When she'd grown old enough to seem like a real girl, he'd built her a house next to his down the path that led to the woods and moved her into it. He didn't want her borrowing his dresses.

Tik Tok lived in a clay house he'd built himself—the most intricate in the village. It was my favorite home to sleep in when I was passing through, because it had the best nooks, and a faerie always likes to sleep in tight places for fear of predators. He'd seen the same constructions done in one of the other tribes on the island—the Bog Dwellers, who lived in the mud bogs among the old bones of prehistoric animals—and he'd dragged the whole rib cage of a beast home piece by piece to make the frame. With a craftsmanship possessed by no one else in any village, he'd fashioned shelves and windows, to create a dwelling that put the rest of the tribe's simple houses to shame.

Now he was sitting by a warm fire inside, as the sun was setting and the night was growing cool, as it often did at the end of the dry season. He wore a long dress of raspberry-dyed leather—his favorite—and his hair braided down his back, a leather thong tied around his head with a peacock feather in back. His posture was straight and graceful as any woman's. His eyes were closed in concentration, and his lips moved in a conversation with the invisible gods that, as shaman, he visited in trances. Out of breath, Tiger Lily moved into the room soundlessly and hovered, waiting for him to finish.

In a village where everything was uniform and tidy, Tik

Tok's house was like a treasure trove. The firelight cast shadows on the curved walls where he kept his curious collection of belongings: tiny bird skulls, feathers, a few stones that looked like any other stones but which he treasured, and a beloved collection of exotic items that had washed ashore over the years, which he had found scouring Neverland's shores. A book, the pages stuck together, the ink blurred. A tarnished metal cup. And, most beloved of all, a box that told time—still ticking away, its mechanism having somehow survived a shipwreck or a long journey across the sea from the continent. The Englanders divided the endlessness of the world into seconds and minutes and hours, and Tik Tok thought this was wonderful.

Tiger Lily moved across the room quietly, examining the clock, the little metal bit he used to wind it, and bending her ear to the loud, steady ticktock, which Tik Tok had renamed himself after in a solemn ceremony attended by the whole village.

Now she sensed a movement, and turned to see that he was observing her.

"Well, my little beast, I hear we have a visitor," he said, looking her up and down with an amused smile. She always managed to look like a wild beast, mud-stained and chaotic. Her hair was constantly escaping her braid to cling to her face, stuck to her, covered in dirt.

"Will we help him?" she asked.

Tik Tok shook his head. "I don't know."

Tiger Lily waited for him to say more, trying her best to remain in respectful silence.

Tik Tok smeared away some of the charcoal he used to line his eyes. "Have you seen my pipe?" he asked.

He stood and moved about the house, searching. He had carved it over two weeks of long intricate work, but it was the fifth one he'd made. He was always losing things. Finally he found it buried under his covers.

He turned his attention to her question, and sighed. Englanders had come to Neverland before. They'd brought their language with them and given it out as a gift to the Bog Dwellers, who had given it to the other tribes in turn over the years. But they'd also brought a strange discomfort to the wild, and they'd been loud and careless in the forest, and gotten themselves murdered by pirates, who hated their fellow Englanders more than anything else on earth and liked to kill them on sight. They'd brought fevers and crippling flus too. But it wasn't any of this that the Sky Eaters feared.

The Englanders had the aging disease. As time went on they turned gray, and shrank, and, inexplicably, they died. It wasn't that Neverlanders didn't know anything about death, but not as a slow giving in, and certainly not an inevitability. This, more than the beasts of their own island, or the brutal pirate inhabitants of the far west shore, was what crept into their dreams at night and chased them through nightmares.

You never could tell when someone would stop growing old in Neverland. For Tik Tok, it had been after wrinkles had walked long deep tracks across his face, but for many people, it was much younger. Some people said it occurred when the most important thing that would ever happen to you triggered something inside that stopped you from moving forward, but Tik Tok thought that was superstition. All anyone knew was that you came to an age and you stayed there, until one day some accident or battle with the dangers of the island claimed you. Therefore sometimes daughters grew older than mothers, and grandchildren became older than grandparents, and age was just a trait, like the color of your hair, or the amount of freckles on your skin.

It was because of the aging disease, Tiger Lily knew, that the Sky Eaters wouldn't want to help the Englander. They didn't want to catch what he had.

But something about the tiny lone figure, floating from one certain death into another, tugged at her—I could hear it. (As a faerie, you can hear when something tugs at someone. It's much like the sound of a low, deep note on a violin string.)

"He won't survive without our help," Tiger Lily said. "We're supposed to be brave, aren't we?" The wrinkles in Tik Tok's face moved in response. The story they told was familiar to her.

"I'm not a stranger to your love of lost causes, dear one. But you have to be careful who you meet," he said, stoking a pipe thoughtfully. "You can't unmeet them." He took a long drag of his pipe. Being near Tik Tok always gave one the feeling that everything in the world was exactly in the place it ought to be, and that rushing through anything would be an insult and a waste. "And you should be thinking of other things. You're getting too old to run wild like you do. Clean yourself up. Brush your hair. Try to look like a girl."

"I will, if you try to look like a man."

He smiled wryly, because they both knew how impossible that was; he didn't have it in him. Tik Tok was as womanly as a man could ever be, and everyone just accepted it, like they accepted the color of the sky, and the fact that night followed the daytime. Grudgingly, he gave Tiger Lily a puff of his pipe. They sat and watched the colors outside the window. From my perch on a shelf, I inhaled the unfurling wisps as they dissipated: the tobacco made the colors thick, the smells richer. Outside, visible through the window, everyone was dispersing from the fire. The girls were walking ahead and the boys were running to catch up. There was, as always, a dance going on between them, one that I'd never seen Tiger Lily take part in.

She lay on her back and pushed her feet against the wall, wiped a layer of sweat from her neck though the air was chilly. She tapped her feet at the wall in a troubled rhythm.

Tik Tok gave her a knowing look. "You're restless. Everything is too small for you, including your own body. That's what it's like to be fifteen. I remember."

There was a noise in the doorway and they both glanced up to see Pine Sap, pale, with Moon Eye behind him looking pensive and sorry, the way she often did.

"They've decided to let the Englander die," he said.

I was asleep on a leaf by the main fire when I heard her come out of her hut.

She went to the river to wash, after everyone else had gone to bed. Crocs sometimes made their way this far inland, but I knew she wasn't as scared of them as some of the others, and that she liked to swim alone, after dark. Following her back to her house, I saw there was one candle burning among the huts. Pine Sap's. He was probably up working on a project, or thinking his deep thoughts. I knew, from nights I'd slept in the village, that he was an insomniac.

When Tiger Lily emerged again from her house and into the square, she'd gathered up a bagful of food.

She set out before the sun came up, her arrows strapped to her back.

I watched her go, intrigued, but also sleepy, comfortable and content. I fell back to sleep before I even thought of following her.

TWO

Before he ran out on me and my mother for a twinkly-eyed nymph named Belladonna, my father told me a few things. He said rotten logs were the best places for mosquitoes. He told me humans weren't to be trusted. And he warned me to stay clear of Peter Pan.

It was when he was tracing for me which parts of the island were forbidden territory, and which weren't. He had called him Pan first. He signaled to me, in a form of language only faeries know: *He can fly. He has horns. He eats men. And he will kill you if he sees you.*

I learned more from the other faeries after that. My childhood friend Mirabella and I used to think about it before bed. We had never seen the lost boys; we didn't know quite what they were—ghosts or demons or living men.

They were the only creatures in the forest we couldn't find to spy on, but they left evidence of themselves: carcasses of beasts and prey in their wake, and sometimes a pirate skull dangling from a tree. They left their tracks everywhere and sometimes left muddy handprints and the occasional curious artifact—like a papier-mâché mask or a tiny wooden sailing ship—to remind us of their presence. Sometimes the wind carried their yells and hoots to us while we lay in our cozy nooks, deep inside rotting hollow logs. They seemed to know the forest better than we did, and we knew the forest like we knew our own wings. These boys were famous for their violence; they were known to eat wild animals raw with their bared teeth, and to steal girls who wandered alone. Imagining what happened to these human girls once they were stolen made me shudder. My father had told me never to go near their territory. Faeries and tribes alike called that part of the forest "Forbidden."

But after my father left, I had the irresistible urge to disobey every rule he'd ever given me. I'd fly all over the area I was supposed to avoid, looking for a thrilling glimpse of the boys, and when I got tired or hungry, I'd make a stop at the Sky Eaters' village nearby, to eat the fleas that can always be found near the animals people keep.

Humans have been known to kill faeries and use us as festive, glowing decorations for certain rituals. But the Sky Eaters and a few other tribes considered the practice barbaric. I rarely felt nervous at all as I sat and ate among them, and it was always fun to observe them. They were colorful, for one thing. The women grew their hair long and fixed it elaborately, and the men—Tik Tok the shaman being the exception—cut theirs short. They had a great tradition of artistry, and made themselves beautiful clothes. They tried to listen to the gods in the trees and the clouds and the water, though they could never hear clearly exactly what they were saying.

It was during one of these visits that I first saw Tiger Lily.

The children were teasing her. That, in itself, wasn't what captured my attention; in the typical village, children are generally almost as cruel as adults. What caught my eye was her stillness. Her absolute stony composure, as if the village could have been burning and she wouldn't have noticed or cared. She was like a dark cloud. She stood, not eight years old yet, black hair disheveled and down to her waist, arms crossed over her chest.

The taunting escalated to pushing until finally a girl, Magnolia Bud, pushed her against a vat of cool, day-old turkey broth, and all the children suddenly joined in to hoist her into the pot, then close the lid down on her. Magnolia Bud then sat on the lid while all the children whispered excitedly to each other and the girl underneath struggled and then went silent. A group of crows nearby got caught up in the excitement and squawked at the children shrilly.

Finally, hearing the commotion, a woman (Aunt Agda, I learned later) appeared, and the children ran away. Not knowing the turkey pot contained a child, she then went off to her chores.

For several moments, there was no sound. And then the lid finally moved, and Tiger Lily climbed out, gasping for breath, shaking and exhausted. She walked home quietly. Tik Tok helped her wipe the broth and strips of turkey from her face. And when Magnolia Bud was found two days later on the village path, having choked to death on a piece of turkey from that night's soup, and with a crow sitting on her hip like an omen, the children—and indeed most of the adults—decided that she was guarded by crows.

Whether that was true or not, I couldn't hear deep enough into her mind to know. But one afternoon, after the children had called her crow girl and run away for fear of her, I watched her slip a raven feather into her hair. After that day, she kept it in.

From then on, I was a goner. A devoted fan. I don't know what Tiger Lily must have thought of me. I didn't seem to be on her mind at all. She must have noticed my increasingly constant presence fluttering along behind her, or up above her, or perching on one of her tassels, but it was as if she accepted me as part of the scenery.

And I wasn't the only one to cling to her unnoticed. There was also Pine Sap. He'd been born skinny and a bit asymmetrical. One of his hazel eyes always seemed to squint a little, making his face appear asymmetrical too. Try as he might, he couldn't work up the bloodlust that made the other boys flourish on hunts—he was always too busy thinking things through. Somehow as children he and Tiger Lily had been shuttled together—both misfits or, as I liked to think of them, strange exotic birds, one too fierce to be hemmed in as a girl, and the other too hesitant to be respected as a boy. Since then, she had never shaken him, though she often tried to. Still, Pine Sap wasn't the type whose ego was wounded easily. His admiration for Tiger Lily was hard and fast and stuck, and failed to waver even when she ignored him completely.

Often when I flew past the village I saw his mother, out in front of their hut calling for him, her dark bushy hair all askew, her voice hoarse from another fight with Pine Sap's father. Pine Sap would arrive, quiet and eyes to the ground, and wait for her to pour her anger onto him. "Look at how crooked you are! You are the shape of those crooked poplars up on the cliffs!" or "How did I produce such a strange creature!" She showed her love for him by trying to shrink him in public and private. And Pine Sap listened calmly, and nodded his head from time to time to let her know she didn't go unheard. It was almost as if he was giving her his silence, so that all of her anger had a place to go. But sometimes, he didn't come when she called, and where was he? Following Tiger Lily through a bog, holding the spiders and reptiles she picked up and absently discarded into his mud-slippery hands, carrying her bow for her like a servant, listening to her grunt and swear over the wrongs people heaped on her. He even listened to more than her sounds, because Tiger Lily was a girl of few words. He listened with his eyes, watched facial expressions, judged body language, and therefore he read Tiger Lily better than anyone else. Perhaps he was drawn to her for this more than any other reason: Pine Sap had a knack for spotting lies from a mile away. And Tiger Lily was the only person he knew who never pretended.

I saw her from time to time as she grew. And as she grew she hunted, she ran, she perfected her aim and her abilities with a paddle. It was like she had an instinctive awareness that she had to do a little something extra to be accepted. For a long time, she took up with the boys, going with them on hunts, dominating in mud fights. Only, she did too well at everything. She was too fast; her aim was too good. Her quiet confidence gave her a reputation for being haughty, and the boys—all except for Pine Sap—didn't like being beaten. So by her thirteenth birthday, they told her that she couldn't join them on hunts anymore. Without a word of complaint, she started hunting alone, in the same areas, and often ran into them with a stag or a rabbit slung over her back while they stood empty-handed.

"That child will spend her life alone," Aunt Agda was fond of saying between cluckings of her tongue, and everyone seemed to agree, except for all the suitors. They began coming from the time Tiger Lily was seven years old (as the shaman's adopted daughter, her rank was coveted). They came from tribes near and far: the Bog Dwellers in the bogs, the Cliff Dwellers who lived in the snowy, pine-covered mountains. Her temper at those times was a spectacle to behold. She chased them all away with a hatchet, murder in her eyes. The hatchet had been a gift from Tik Tok, though he hadn't meant it for that purpose. (Aunt Fire, one of the matrons, had even suggested her own son, Giant, as Tiger Lily's ideal mate, but everyone had only tittered at that, because Giant was an oaf.)

Usually, though, Tiger Lily saved her inner rage for the defense of lost causes. Such as when the boys bullied Pine Sap, who always seemed too puzzled to retaliate. Or when children taunted Aunt Fire for her wrinkles, though Aunt Fire was no friend to Tiger Lily. She'd knocked two boys unconscious in a spat over Moon Eye, and people said she'd hit both of them with one blow. She even defended *me* once, though it may have been coincidental. Stone was trying to kill me to make a night-light for his hut. He had cornered me in a crevice of rock, and was just moving for the blow when Tiger Lily appeared out of nowhere, hatchet in hand, and petrified him into backing away. It was the first time I ever thought she might know I existed. But her mind was so dark right then, I never knew for sure. Anyway, whether she'd meant to save me didn't matter. She was the most interesting girl I had ever seen, and I couldn't resist staying near her to see what happened next.

*   *   *

A village, one as orderly as the Sky Eaters', wants its members to fit just so. Tiger Lily didn't, and so gossip followed her. By the time she was fifteen, the age she was the day of the shipwreck, opinions by the dozen landed in each hollow track left by her feet. I could hear the thoughts flying overhead, or when I was perched in a hay roof letting myself be groomed by crickets. It was rumored among the young people that at night she became her crow spirit, and they dared each other to leave piles of stones outside her door as a feat of bravery, fearing that they might peer through her window and see only a crow staring back at them. She would collect the stones the following morning, bewildered. Fear and, yes, even a bit of envy of her wild independence followed her side by side. But if she ever turned into a crow and flew away on night adventures, I never saw it.

Still, the longer I was around her, the more I could see the colors of her mind and the recesses of her heart. There was a beast in there. But there was also a girl who was afraid of being a beast, and who wondered if other people had beasts in their hearts too. There was strength, and there was also just the determination to look strong. She guarded herself like a secret.

But now—even having watched her for years—I could still be surprised by her. I was carrying some clover home at dusk, and just passing the council fire when there was a buzz among the villagers, and a shadowy figure appeared. It sent the well-organized group around the fire into a shudder, and a few carefully perched bowls into the fire. She'd approached so quietly they hadn't noticed her. She was so dirty that it took a moment to recognize her.

Her arms were piled with foreign items—a telescope, a glass, and a little wooden box. She dropped the load and stared at everyone with her inscrutable eyes, her crow feather cocked at an angle.

Standing there, hair pasted to her back, covered in sweat, blood on her shoulders where a freshly killed rabbit lay, arrows pointing above her head, she was a triumphant and fearsome sight. No one could have guessed the way her heart pounded.

"I've saved the Englander," she said. Everyone scattered.

THREE

T he following dusk, the familiar music of Pine Sap's mother berating him with words like "you're a mistake" and "you are just like a girl" drifted through the village. The Sky Eaters tried to respect each other's privacy, but at times like these, some curled in their toes and ground their teeth in frustration and pity. One or two even chuckled cynically and muttered that it would build Pine Sap's character. Tiger Lily found him on the path near the dusty chicken yard, feeding the baby chicks.

He looked up at her. As she took a step forward, he stopped.

"Don't worry, I won't get too close," she said. All day Tiger Lily had been watching her hands, looking for signs of aging. Sifting through her long black hair looking for grays. Everyone in the village seemed to have adopted the same notion. Walking to and from the central square, or past her on the paths, they parted way for her like she was a cold breeze, afraid of catching the aging disease now that she had been with an Englander. They whispered about Tik Tok having let her run wild for as long as he had, and how that had contributed to her betrayal. Everyone was part of the debate on how she should be punished. But so far, she had managed to ignore them all. Except Tik Tok, who wore a dark face and a darker mood as he made his visits around the village, delivering medicine, saying the necessary chants, and simply sitting to listen to those who needed an ear. It wasn't like him to be angry, and Tiger Lily had watched him with guilt.

"I'm not worried," Pine Sap said. Then he looked back down at the chicks. "Their mother takes such good care of them, doesn't she?" he said, gesturing toward the mother hen, who stood proudly above her brood, picking up worms for them.

A current of compassion moved through Tiger Lily. And the momentary impulse to go terrorize Pine Sap's mother. She wanted to tell him something encouraging, but the words wouldn't come to her. She looked down the path thoughtfully, and was surprised to see Aunt Fire leaning on a fence and looking at her, a strange smile playing on her lips.

I had grown to dislike Aunt Fire over the years, almost as much as I disliked her oafish son, Giant. Her mind was a blur of bold colors and bright malice. And Giant's house—the fence of which Aunt Fire was leaning on now—was one of the only ones I wouldn't sleep in, because of the horrible noises and smells the man produced in his sleep. He would be seen sometimes sitting outside, sucking his teeth, picking out the pieces of crumbs and examining them, or eyeing the girls. He had grown into his fiftieth year before his aging had stopped. Everyone suspected his taciturn disposition of keeping him aging for so long—after all, when you were that cantankerous, it was hard for something important to happen to you. At fifty, his brother was eaten by a beast while out hunting, and that seemed to be the same time that Giant finally stopped aging for good.

The village was small, but there were big personalities that set it wobbling, and Aunt Fire and her son were two of those. They were tolerated because everyone born to the tribe was part of a family, for better or for worse. The matron's gaze made Tiger Lily feel unsettled and hemmed in.

"Bend?" she asked Pine Sap.

"Yes." He just started walking, and she fell in step beside him.

They walked to the river bend, stripped down, and waded in. It was their secret, because the village would have been in an uproar at a boy and girl swimming naked together, even two as much like siblings as Tiger Lily and Pine Sap. In the water, unlike on land, Pine Sap was graceful. He kept his distance from her, and she was careful not to go near him.

"What was the Englander like?" Pine Sap asked.

"He had no hair. He was very sick," she said. Pine Sap couldn't have been hoping for much more; Tiger Lily wasn't one for sharing. "I need to get back to him."

The village council and, more importantly, Tik Tok, had forbidden her to go anywhere until they decided how to punish her.

"And now they're all scared to touch me," she said. "They should be, I guess."

Pine Sap twisted onto his back to float. Tiger Lily noticed that in the water, unencumbered by the weight of his body, Pine Sap was as good a swimmer as anyone.

Alighting on a floating leaf, I dipped a toe into the water; with the night growing cool, it felt warm and inviting, but I didn't go in for fear of getting waterlogged and stuck to its shining surface. Many a stronger faerie than me had drowned in that way.

The village, slices of it visible up through the trees, gave an orange, flickering glow from the many fires. The sounds of talking echoed down the hill, as did the smell of meat roasting on the main fire.

Tiger Lily was trying to say something, but had to think several moments before she did. "You're not a mistake," she finally offered.

Pine Sap waded. "Thanks. I know. I just . . . I don't know what else to do but be patient with her. Everyone has their own reasons for being the way they are, I guess."

He looked so sad that Tiger Lily provoked him into a race.

They splashed back and forth across the river, and then sat at the water's edge and ate some berries Tiger Lily found. Panting, they ate, Tiger Lily ravenously.

It had become a habit for her to spend hours with Pine Sap like this, even though she didn't think she cared for him much. It was as if he were a piece of herself that she couldn't misplace for very long. I hovered near his shoulder. In the dusk his squinty hazel eyes took on a pale gleam that looked like tiny candle flames. The sparkle of it gave him the appearance of being in on a joke that no one understood but him.

They dried off carefully, and as they walked up, they passed Tik Tok. He barely looked at them.

All through dinner, the villagers made sure to sit far from Tiger Lily. Many people wouldn't even look at her, for fear they could catch aging through their eyes. Only Aunt Fire seemed to study her unblinkingly and without fear.

The next morning, Tiger Lily was up before dawn, braiding her hair sloppily and inserting her crow feather, and I was up catching my breakfast among the bugs that hovered around the light of her lantern. The morning light brought noise and activity, and the peace of the predawn vanished rapidly. When the sun was just peaking the treetops I followed her out to go sit by the fire with the women and girls, as Tik Tok had recently been urging her to do.

As she sat, they all moved down their logs and scuttled closer together. They would have protested if she weren't Tik

Tok's daughter, but Tik Tok was a man who, present or not, commanded their respect. The smell of dust and grass and dry leaves floated on the air.

Aunt Agda, Aunt Sticky Feet, and Aunt Fire were the matrons at the fire. Aunt Sticky Feet was so named because of the time she'd walked through hot tar and gotten her foot stuck to a chicken that had run in front of her a moment later. A feather had burned itself into her foot permanently, making her sole a living fossil. Aunt Agda was a kind woman, younger looking than the other two but in actuality much older. She was self-conscious by nature, but always willing to help anyone with anything. Aunt Fire, still glancing at Tiger Lily in the strange, satisfied way she had the night before, was the ringleader, witty, full of information (it didn't matter if it was accurate or not—she always said it with such confidence that it seemed true).

"Here." Aunt Agda reached out timidly and put a basket of thread at Tiger Lily's side, making sure not to touch her.

"Our little death bird," Aunt Fire said, pulling her thread through her suede blanket and barely looking up. Her wedding bracelets jangled against each other—a reminder of her long-dead husband, killed by beasts. "I thought birds were supposed to be beautiful," she said with a wry smile at the other women, then bit her thread to break it. Long ago, Aunt Fire's delicate features had gotten lost in the folds of her skin, so that her face gave the appearance of having been mashed against a hard surface and left that way. The other women seemed to bristle at her icy comments, but kept their thoughts to themselves. It simply caught, like yawning.

Some of the younger girls tittered. Tiger Lily turned her face down to her work. She was making a belt. The strings were all tangled up and her colors clashed. Her fingers moved like hunks of meat. Across the circle, Moon Eye gave her a lone sympathetic smile. In contrast to Tiger Lily's, Moon Eye's work was intricate and beautiful, her dainty hands moving like little grasshoppers, fleet and sure. She was a wisp of a thing. Sitting there, so delicate and dreamy, she looked as if someone had only given half a life to her. It was whispered among the tribe she wouldn't live long, she was so tiny and thin, with feather-like fingers and a crackling voice. Next to her, the other young girls wove with deft hands, though their designs were much more formulaic and less imaginative than Moon Eye's.

The women weighed in with their own thoughts of what should be done with Tiger Lily.

"Could have been worse," Aunt Agda said, low and soft and barely audible. "Could have been the lost boys." This brought ghastly smiles from the youngsters. Aunt Skip Pebble hissed and spat in a gesture of superstition. Several of the women snapped their fingers in excitement in the peculiar gesture of the tribe. But they were also all a little breathless. The lost boys figured in a favorite story for scaring the younger children, and for scaring themselves. It was like they were drawn to the idea of the monsters lurking in the woods, and at the same time horrified by it. I, too, felt my heart beat a little faster.

"What you did was very brave," Aunt Sticky Feet said, her words clipped but not unkind, "but men don't want women who are brave. They want women who make them feel like men."

"I don't care about that," Tiger Lily said quietly. The girls laughed and the women all fell awkwardly silent for a while as they worked, except for Aunt Fire, who was never self-aware enough to feel awkward.

"Tik Tok was born to be two genders," Aunt Fire said tightly. "That's the way he was made. But you're a girl. Someday you'll want to be a prisoner to someone other than yourself."

Tiger Lily stared down at her work and chose not to reply.

They were just finishing up when Tik Tok emerged from his house and walked over. His heart was so heavy that everyone could feel the weight of it, and the hairs prickled on the backs of their necks. The boys, finished and exhausted from their games, came to hover.

Tik Tok looked like he hadn't slept, and like he had something to say. Everyone grew quiet.

"Tiger Lily, we've decided that since you've already been exposed, you can return to visit the Englander, if he's still alive, and learn what you can for us."

Tik Tok sank slightly here. He looked tired, worn down, and defeated. "But people in the village have suggested you've run wild too long." Curiously, his eyelids began to tremble, as if the tiny muscles had gone weak, and his eyes became glassy with tears. Tiger Lily, who had never seen Tik Tok so distraught, was struck with a sudden, burning fear. "As shaman, I've decided you are to be married." He looked around the circle and his eyes rested on Aunt Fire, then trailed back to Tiger Lily almost involuntarily. "You'll be married to Giant at the end of the hot season."

Aunt Fire's glance showed itself for what it was: triumph. Of all the people sitting at the fire, she was the only one unsurprised by the news.

Tiger Lily went as still as if she were prey and her life depended on blending with her surroundings. But for the widening of eyes, the opening and gasping of lips, *everyone* was still. There was only one real movement. One figure moved next to Tiger Lily, and one set of fingers slipped themselves between her own.

No one seemed to notice that Pine Sap had taken his life into his hands by holding hers.

FOUR

I moved into the village permanently that week. Up till then, I'd been shuttling my things from here to there, never sleeping in the same place more than a few days in a row. But now I felt the need to stay close to Tiger Lily. I don't know if I thought I could protect her or if I just needed to see how it would end for her. But somehow it felt important to be there. Faeries can be unfailingly loyal, even, apparently, to someone who doesn't seem to notice them. And I felt loyal to the girl with the crow feather in her hair.

Aunt Fire wasted no time putting Tiger Lily to work, now that she was going to be her mother-in-law. She forbade Tiger Lily's rambles in the woods, and her solitary hunts. She made her take on chores for both herself and her son, though Tiger Lily had never even been good at keeping her own house and clothes in order. The one thing Aunt Fire couldn't forbid was Tiger Lily's return to the Englander.

Tiger Lily caught sight of Giant on her way out of the village the next morning, for the first time since their engagement.

When Giant had stopped aging, his growth in years seemed to have been replaced with a spurt in outward growth: he was enormous—every bit of him. It was easy to mistake him for a boulder walking through the village; sometimes that seemed more believable than that the shape coming toward you was actually a man. He met her gaze now, his eyes dull. The only acknowledgment he gave her was to suck his teeth in her general direction. As she walked away from him, the village's pity trailed her, the same way their fear always had.

She entered the woods in a daze. I heard wisps of her bewilderment with each breath she took as she walked, and even smelled it in the breeze after it ruffled her hair. In Neverland, the year was divided into three seasons: the dry, followed by the wet, and then the hot season, when everything bloomed and grew in the humid heat. The end of the hot season was nine full moons away. She hadn't yet come to fully grasp what it meant or how largely things had changed, and how in nine moons she would be married. Most of all, she couldn't understand Tik Tok.

It was an hour's walk to her destination. The house where she had left the Englander was a remnant of visiting missionaries who—unable to cope with the heat and the beasts and the pirates—had died somewhere in the forest. The roof still stood intact, along with three of the stone walls, but the fourth had crumbled badly from years of the harsh wind. From the house's back window there was a view of the ocean beyond Neverland, and below, hungry waves lapped against a thin slip of coastline. Wind buffeted the house constantly; in the rainy season it could be deadly. All in all, the place was windswept and lonely.

The house smelled musty and the coolness stroked Tiger Lily's cheeks. Against one wall was a rough cot with a straw mattress. There, in a lump, lay the Englander. His bald head glinted in the dim light. He blinked at us from behind a pair of crooked but intact spectacles, but didn't move or say a word. Tiger Lily unwrapped the food she'd brought and sat at the edge of his bed, and tried to feed him, but he wouldn't eat. She checked his ankle, which she'd bandaged to stabilize a broken bone. She'd bandaged his chest too, but was unsure how many ribs he'd broken. She poured some water into his mouth. Then she sat and watched him, and waited. He slept, on and on.

Listless and eager for a task, she soon made the difficult climb down to the beach to gather the many things that had washed ashore, making the immense physical effort to pack them up to the house while I hid among the branches that overhung the cliffs, watching for the hawks who liked to scan the edges of the ocean for prey. A canvas trunk. Some clothes. The bodies had disappeared, eaten by sharks or taken by mermaids to use the bones for their dwellings in the deep.

When she returned, she sat in the darkness awhile longer, waiting and listening. And then simply went to work. She pounded a clay-and-hay mixture to stuff into the holes in the walls to protect against the wind. She sweated and cooked and dried food and belongings.

The Englander was awake the next time I looked, and he watched her come and go. He had begun to eat. His round cheeks puffed out and he stuttered one word, his lips shaking: "Phillip." He held a frail hand to his chest.

She laid her hand on her own chest and said, "Tiger Lily."

"A ship will come looking for us," he said, with effort. He licked his lips a few times, then nodded, reassuring himself. He reached out and patted Tiger Lily's hand. She didn't flinch.

I wondered about the man's ship. Neverland was so deeply and snugly tucked into a remote corner of the Atlantic, so far from anything else of interest and so surrounded by violent and usually impassable tides and currents, that the ships that did end up here usually only did so by accident. To find the island on purpose, I'd heard pirates claim over the years, was next to impossible. The pirates themselves had stumbled upon the island long ago during an escape, and now sheltered in a cove on the remote northwest side in between raids on the far-off trade routes.

Tiger Lily opened a trunk, its contents surprisingly,

immaculately dry. She pulled out a few books, which, to her, contained only nonsensical symbols.

Phillip made an eager gesture and muttered, "Take it." He made an attempt at an encouraging smile. "It's a wonderful book. You deserve it." Tiger Lily stared at the cover, then at him unsurely. "Do you know how to read?" he asked. She shook her head. She didn't, but Tik Tok did. He had tried to teach her, years before, but she had had no patience for it.

As it grew dark, Tiger Lily built a fire. She tried to imagine where the Englander had come from, but all the world outside the island seemed impossible, like a story. I hid behind a log to stand close to the flames and watch them dance. I played with the sparks, throwing them against pebbles.

Finally, she squatted by Phillip's bed to say good-bye. "I'll come back," she said. "I promise you, I'll look after you," He nodded. Just as she was about to stand, he pushed something into her hands. A tiny box that had come out of one of the trunks. Inside was a thin gold necklace, with an ornate gold pendant that held a small pearl dangling at its end. "You should have it." His brown eyes lit up for a moment, from behind his spectacles. He licked his lips, swallowed. "It was my wife's. It's precious to me." Again, his cracked lips widened in a frail smile.

Tiger Lily held the necklace, deeply curious. While old shells washed in all the time, she'd never seen a pearl before. The necklace was the most exquisite object she'd ever held. Wincing, Phillip rested his hands on his stomach. He was a portly man, but clearly malnourished now. "Don't lose it," he said. And made a feeble attempt at a smile. Tiger Lily hung the necklace around her neck.

Out in the open, it had cooled off a little, but the air still felt wet and warm when we set off just before dusk.

She made her way down the hill to the edge of the woods, holding the book, which she planned to give to Tik Tok. Her thoughts turned back to the village.

The sky fell away as she entered the thick of the forest, and I had flown up high to get a good look at the stars. She was soon wrapped in a cocoon of night noises . . . insects nibbling on plants or chirping, leaves rustling. The still, thick heat wrapped us in a fine layer of sweat, and Tiger Lily was tying her long black braids up to the back of her head when a low voice caught her ears, close enough to startle her.

She hid instantly, holding her body close to a tree, its rough life breathing beneath her hands. Then, gauging the voice's location, she moved on toward it, utterly silent, her senses sharp. She didn't notice she'd wandered into the tangled lowlands of the forbidden territory until afterward, when it was too late.

Almost immediately, she came to a deep, black lagoon. She stopped short at the water's edge.

She waited for several minutes, and was about to turn around and continue home, when there was a movement among the branches to her left.

In the dark, I could barely see him. He was covered in mud, and blended in with the trees. He had an ungainly walk, like something unconscious of itself. His hair was caked in dirt and none of his features were visible, except his eyes glinted in the glow of the moonlight, and I got a yellow-lit glimpse of his features: a pale face, smooth and animate. He wasn't terribly large in frame. There was a delicateness to his shoulders; they were like chicken wings. Below me, Tiger Lily was frozen as well.

A baby was tucked beside him in the shadows. The baby cooed.

Clearly, he hadn't seen us yet. He was working on something, and I could see as my eyes adjusted that it was a spear.

I had never seen a creature like him. He was nothing like the men of the villages—orderly and well-postured, dignified and stiff. Nor was he like the men of tribes across the island—the Cliff Dwellers or the Bog Dwellers. He seemed very young, and also fragile.

And then there was a muddy, wet sound behind him. He turned, and as he did, I studied the sweeping black lagoon he now faced, still and mirrorlike under the moon. And then a bubble from the surface, and a figure slithered out of the dark water. Effortlessly, it beached itself on a rock protruding not far from the shore. A patch of moonlight coming through the clouds raked over it, revealing half of a woman—a mermaid. Her long hair was wet and pasted to her back. She waved at him in the dark, and he waved back. He walked over to the water, and said something in a low voice, and she laughed. He took another step toward the water's edge. And she said his name.

"Pan."

Below me, Tiger Lily startled. The tree shook, almost imperceptibly, in her arms. It was nothing. But enough for him to sense she was there. He lifted his face up, his glittering eyes. Tiger Lily ducked behind a tree and disappeared, and I fluttered up into the branches.

He moved toward us.

I watched from above as he hunted her. I could hear him breathing, listening for whatever it was that was hiding from him. Tiger Lily set her sights on a tree a few feet away, and came silently out, hiding behind the next. She chose another tree, and again, ran toward it on silent feet. They waited each other out. He disappeared into the trees beyond a small clearing to her left. She took the opportunity to veer right, behind a boulder. And in this way, they zigzagged toward the edge of the forbidden territory, where the scrubby, tangled lowlands gave way to high ground and taller trees. Her feet found the bare spots between rocks and over branches. And then she was beyond the line of low swampy growth and rising into familiar territory.

She knew how to fade into this forest. Long afterward, I heard him walking back and forth through the trees, but we slipped along the shadows, and in this way made the slow journey home, arriving long after nightfall.

FIVE

Tik Tok closed the book that Tiger Lily had brought. His hair was a revelation this morning, a glossy braid he had started on at dawn, woven with tiny seashells. He put the book on the shelf right next to his clock. He had been reading it many hours at a time for days. "I love it," he said. "Thank you again." He seemed to be bearing up the weight of the air as he stood, slow and tired. "Are you ready?"

Tiger Lily nodded.

Since she had been a child, Tik Tok had often taken her with him on his gathering expeditions, saying that he needed one person to help. But secretly, it was their private time to just be together in comfortable silence. Now, the silence was thick and tense. Tiger Lily was confused and hurt, but she preferred to stay that way rather than question him.

She kept her mouth closed as they walked, so that none of her anger would tumble out. Besides her clandestine swims with Pine Sap, she had never kept anything from Tik Tok. She avoided his eyes, and kept her gaze on his heels as he took the lead.

Tik Tok shambled along in front of her as they entered the forest. From behind, he was shaped like an eggplant, his hips swaying under his deep-green tunic, the shells in his hair bright in the morning sun.

After several minutes, they knelt in the dead leaves and rooted around.

Today they were looking for taro root, which Tik Tok used to treat insect bites.

"It's for the best if the Englander dies," he said. "Better than him suffering longer."

Tiger Lily swallowed. She had been to the house twice since our first visit together, and Phillip didn't seem to be getting any better. Clearly, Tik Tok thought she was holding out false hope. But hope wasn't exactly what it was. She, too, believed the man was doomed, and she couldn't explain to herself why she kept going back. She pulled at the taro root fiercely, holding it up in clumps.

"If he dies, it was all for nothing," she said. Tik Tok winced, and she hurried to change the subject. "Do you really need all of this?" she asked.

"You always want to be prepared," he said. "You don't want someone to come to you needing help, and you can't give it because you didn't gather that herb."

I had watched Tik Tok minister his potions to almost every person in the village: the old and young, the meddling, the generous and the petty, equally. I alone had seen him sitting up nights with those with fevers, sitting patiently next to people covered in salves for burns or cuts or animal bites, when Tiger Lily had tried to stay awake and fallen asleep, strong willed, but still a child after all. Twice, I had seen him nurse people back from the brink of death in secret, so the rest of the tribe wouldn't think the person was weak. And once he had slaved over Giant himself for four nights, who had never been nice to anyone, least of all Tik Tok. He would sit there, his wrinkled face immovable, his eyes steady. I'd often stayed awake in my nook as long as I could, until my eyes drooped, and more than once, I'd fallen asleep behind his clock, and I'd woken to find him still wide-awake beside his patient. His collections—including the clock I slept behind—and his hair were his only indulgences, the sole things he did for himself.

Now I watched his face as he and Tiger Lily worked. It was a fine, delicate, feminine face, with full lips and warm brown eyes. His movements were unconscious but always minced, small, womanly.

"It's my fault," he said suddenly, the words seeming to bubble out of their silent work. "I wanted you. That was my mistake. I knew I'd never have a child. I begged them to let me keep you, though for a man to take in a little girl

42

is unheard of. To take any child who isn't a Sky Eater is unheard of. As eldest woman, it was Aunt Fire's decision to let me or not. So she made me give her a promise. When it was time for you to marry, you should marry her son. It was a secret. She wanted it to seem like I chose Giant. To marry the daughter of the shaman would bring him great respect."

Tik Tok leaned back on his heels and looked up, wiping a stray hair from his forehead delicately. "I was always able to put her off. The tribe wouldn't get behind her. Until this. The Englander and everything." He sighed. "It's not your fault. It was my selfishness. I didn't have the courage to leave you in the woods. But I should have let someone else have you . . . one of the other tribes," he said. He leaned down onto one palm as, with the other, he yanked a root from the ground and brushed it off. "I could have told you. But I didn't want you to live under a shadow. I never held you back from anything."

Tiger Lily was silent for a while, her long, dark hair falling across her face, obscuring her expression, and Tik Tok stared at the root in his hands. Finally she reached for his fingers. "I'm glad you took me. It's just a husband. Maybe it won't be terrible."

"It was my job to protect you," he said. "And I didn't."

Tiger Lily shook her head. "You have. I'm okay. Really, Tik Tok." Secretly, Tiger Lily knew it was her job to protect him too.

Tik Tok smiled, but his eyes became wet. His shoulders

43

sank, and he steadied himself where he knelt over a patch of bitter gourd.

"I let you down, little one."

She reached for his arm. "I'm not so little. I can take care of myself."

"Yes, I know." He frowned. "But you shouldn't have to. You should have someone to love and take care of you. Not like him."

Tiger Lily didn't want someone to take care of her. But I heard the longing in Tik Tok's heart too, and the loneliness of being such a singular type of person, without another like himself to hold at night. He didn't want the same for his daughter.

"You love me," she said. "That's enough. We love each other."

"Yes. Yes, that's true." He smiled. "We are a love story."

That night from my perch, I heard something behind the house, like footsteps, circling from behind the cover of the woods. But when I looked out, there was nothing there.

SIX

I've seen Tiger Lily move through the forest as a deadly predator, duck easily through briar patches and over boulders, this fallen rock, that noisy leaf, under that branch, so silently it seemed she was made of air. But I'd never seen her so intent on something as she was on the stone house.

She returned there whenever she could. The moment she finished weaving leggings for Giant, or scraping the dead skin off Aunt Fire's toes, she would disappear into the trees, without anyone really noticing she was gone. For a while I was too busy to follow her, dealing with some faeries from back home who came to try to convince me to return where I belonged. When they finally left and I did have time to go with her, I noticed that on the walk both ways, we peered into the trees, always thinking of Pan, and wondering whether he was somewhere there watching us.

But the trips were worth it, because Phillip was improving. We had found him this last time sitting up in bed and peeling a star apple from a bunch Tiger Lily had left for him. He'd greeted us with a strong voice. "I'll be out of bed soon," he promised sheepishly. "Then you won't have to wait on me all the time." Tiger Lily had left with a smile.

That night, just approaching the fire in the main square, she was startled when she saw that Aunt Fire was waiting for her, her sagging body lit by the light of the flames, where several of the villagers were gathered, digesting their food and talking their way into sleepiness before they went off to bed. They all looked up as Tiger Lily approached.

Aunt Fire stepped close to her, holding something behind her back. In a flash, she pulled it out, and struck Tiger Lily across the face with a bamboo cane.

Tiger Lily fell backward, and the people around the fire went silent.

"You belong to me, and your duties will be to take care of my son. Not straggling home late at night. I need you to myself for the next few days. No house in the woods."

She hobbled off to bed.

The last of the dry season passed. When the first rains started arriving, the way to the house on the cliffs was impassable. Every afternoon a fog fell on the whole island, and threatened to swallow it up. We were unable to return to the stone house for six days. It was too long.

SEVEN

Tiger Lily was trying to work on a water pouch for Giant that Aunt Fire had demanded she make. She kept on peering up at Pine Sap and Moon Eye over her work, her eyebrows knitted darkly. Her work was a mere shadow of Moon Eye's, and for some reason, it embarrassed her for Pine Sap to see it.

I was in the rafters dealing with troubles of my own. I was carrying a raindrop to keep in a little hole in the wood, so I could drink from it at my leisure. But each raindrop I lifted kept falling apart. Water is so delicate.

Tiger Lily worked stoically on her pouch as if sewing was the worst thing to have ever befallen anyone.

Then, outside, there was a shift in the sounds of the village. The women all looked at each other, surprised and on alert.

Suddenly, Stone poked his wet face in through the window.

"Pirates," he said breathlessly, the rain dripping down his cheeks and eyelids, and hurried away.

They were all up in a moment and out of the hut into the deluge. I flew out toward where a crowd of men and boys had gathered near the front entrance of the village. The women and girls were all retreating to the houses. Tik Tok directed Tiger Lily to do the same. But as soon as he stopped looking, she followed behind him.

Before the braves stood a ragtag crew of men, in torn, scraggled clothes.

Tiger Lily slowly sidled up beside Tik Tok, silently, and he made an unconscious, protective gesture to hold her back. It was the only movement he made that evinced any fear or discomfort. There was a truce between the pirates and the Sky Eaters, based on the agreement that neither side wanted trouble from the other. But there was little trust between them.

"We don't know about the boys," Tik Tok was saying. "We hear sounds sometimes. Nothing more."

The pirates' captain was not a large man. Yet the others were clearly in thrall to him, their bodies turned toward him nervously. His wavy black hair was just going gray; he had high bony cheeks, and a piece of old, stained cloth tied around his head to hold back his hair. The whole group stank of sourness, old spirits, and filth.

"We would very much like to find them," the captain said politely.

"We cannot help you, friend."

The captain smiled; it broke through his lips and stayed there, masklike. "No, of course not. Yes, okay."

They turned to go, and shuffled a few feet backward. Suddenly the captain seemed to remember something, or sense something, and he swiveled, only instead of facing Tik Tok again, he trained his gaze on Tiger Lily. His eyes were flat disks, bloodshot around the empty blue, and they studied the braiding in her hair, grazed her neck, and settled on her necklace. "That's lovely; did someone give that to you?" he asked. Tik Tok took a protective step toward Tiger Lily. She stared at the pirate silently. "It looks English," he said, bemused. He smiled again, and I felt the smile in my fingers and in the soles of my feet; it invaded me like a bad spirit, and Tiger Lily shivered. As he turned, his flat eyes scanned the ground, so subtly it was barely noticeable. But only barely. Tiger Lily saw.

"Well, thank you for your time." He seemed pleased.

It was later that day, sitting around the women's circle in the drying hut, that suddenly Tiger Lily jolted. And in that one moment, I knew what she did.

EIGHT

The leaves cut at her face. Her breath came in gasps. Even in her mad rush, she leaped the rocks without missing a step. She was at the bottom of the rise when she saw the smoke. I didn't fly ahead of her. I stuck to her shoulder, and in her state she never knew I was there.

The trunks were in the front yard, burning. The house had been torn apart, even the walls knocked down. The Englander was gone. Tiger Lily searched the ground for the path they'd taken, and her eyes followed footprints to the cliff's edge, and a shudder ran through her.

She knew what lay below. Pirates.

Tiger Lily sank onto the rocky ledge. The ocean was at high tide and crashed right against the rocks. It had washed away whatever the pirates had thrown onto the shore.

She stood. She followed their tracks. A cooler head would have remembered the truce.

Pirates were fierce adversaries, but they weren't stealthy ones. With little effort, and within half a mile, we were close enough that I could hear them up ahead.

One man, balding and slow, straggled behind the others. He was muttering to himself compulsively.

Tiger Lily had her arm around his neck before he knew she was behind him, and had him against a tree. Her knife was at his throat, and she moved to slice, but first she looked in his eyes, to let him know of his death. And she paused. He was crying. By the redness of his eyes and face, she could tell he'd been crying for some time.

She watched the tears in wonder.

He didn't say a word. No one turned to come back for him—or even paused on their way, not noticing he was gone.

Hovering behind her, I could see where Tiger Lily's pulse throbbed. The tears ran over the knuckles of the hand that held his neck.

And she couldn't make her hand move to kill him. She let go. He fell back against the tree, and down onto his hands and knees, then recovered himself and looked up at her. He turned and lunged into the woods, and she let him go.

She staggered the other way, back toward the stone house.

She wasn't herself. She left such easy footprints in the mud. She didn't look behind her, keep her mind on her peripheral vision like all Sky Eaters were taught to do. She stumbled through the woods, and she didn't hear him behind her until he had his arm around her waist. She bucked. They slammed against a tree. She kicked and kicked. But it was too late.

Peter Pan dragged her into the bushes.

NINE

In the chaos, I didn't see him tie her. I bit him, but he, quick as a blink, grasped me between his fingers and flicked me away. Then forgot me as he turned back to Tiger Lily.

Tiger Lily tried to stand and dizziness brought her down again. She tried to move her hands but they were tied behind her back. He reached for her neck, took her pearl between his fingers, then, with a flash of his dagger, sliced the chain from where it had rested against her collarbone and tied it around his own. I flew back at him and bit him, right at the shoulder. He flicked me off again, barely noticing. I landed in a grapevine, tangled and winded.

He knelt in front of her, slowly and quietly, and from above, I couldn't tell whether it was to slit her throat. He held her chin and looked at her face.

"Are you a boy or a girl?"

She blinked at him. His face was mud covered, making his eyes glitter in the gritty mask of dirt he wore. His hair was matted to his skull. Suddenly his teeth showed through his lips in a smile.

She didn't reply. The rain was abating, and dripped loudly on the giant leaves above. She butted her head into his teeth. He let out a deep, guttural moan.

I expected him to kill her then, but he only stared at her and rubbed his lip in surprise. Blood flowed down his chin, but it was the surprise that held him there, staring at her. And then he laughed.

"Boy, I guess.

"You're sad about that man," he said. It wasn't a question. "I've seen you, watching over him. I thought you were a girl at first. But you're too strong. I thought about stopping it sooner. It's too close to our woods," he said. "It's good they took care of him."

Tiger Lily sucked in her breath. Her chin sank against her chest.

Pan paused, studying her stricken face. He seemed to be thinking over his words, though I couldn't tell for sure. I'd never tried to listen to someone whose thoughts were so muddled.

Suddenly, he darted off. Tiger Lily tried to stand, and failed. In a moment he was back with a handful of spotted yellow orchids, sloppy and pulled up at the roots, which he laid in a pile. Underneath the mud, around the circles of his eyes, his skin was pale. Soft as velvet to look at. His eyes were blue.

He knelt before the flowers, so suddenly solemn that it appeared he was making a joke. Tiger Lily stared at him, bewildered. He still had the delicateness we had seen at the lagoon, but he must have been deceptively strong, because when he pulled her beside him, she went easily, like a doll. He made her kneel. "We should have a funeral," he said.

Pan held his hands clasped in a tent on his lap, and he bowed his head.

He seemed to be trying to recall something, and it was a long time before he finally said, "Our Father. Our Father. Our Father. Amen."

Then he leaned back, and his face was blank again. He smiled, all white teeth. "There."

A piercing cry rose from somewhere in the woods behind him. Tiger Lily pushed herself back harder against her tree.

"Just the mermaids," he said. "The moon's rising."

He did something curious then. He wiped something off his knife that might have been blood. And then he carved a few words into the tree just behind the flowers. It took several minutes, but he was meticulous about each letter. IN MEMRY OF THE STRANJER, it said. HE LIVD AND DID. He turned and smiled at her.

Tiger Lily shimmied her wrists. It was the twitching that gave her away.

Peter's face grew grim and perplexed. He reached for her wrists. It was the wrong thing to do.

For all the time I had watched over Tiger Lily, I still underestimated her. She must have been free for some time, because as he leaned in, she flung all her rage against him with her weight, held him against a tree, her fingers around his neck. Panting, her heart racing, she squeezed until he choked for breath and sank slowly down the tree, half conscious.

She left him dazed and lying in the dirt, and ran.

It wasn't until the next day that Tiger Lily realized she'd left her necklace behind, hanging around his neck.

TEN

Peter didn't love Tiger Lily the first time he saw her, or even the second or the third. But Reginald Smee did. How did I know? Because I didn't follow Tiger Lily home that night. I followed the pirates instead.

I made the night journey across the island, trailing the clipped leaves and muddy prints that announced the way the pirates had gone. The forest at night is different from the forest in the day. As a faerie, you can't slip through it unnoticed, because you give off a faint glow that is like a beacon in the dark, deep Neverland nights. But we are equipped with defenses too. Great speed. Excellent eyesight. Sly, secretive natures that lend themselves to seeking the best hiding places. And the pirates, while deadly, were careless enough not to notice me.

They camped about halfway to the cove and ate dinner by a warm fire. I watched them from the cold, gritty shelter of a crevice in a rock nearby. And I learned about Smee, the man Tiger Lily had spared because of his tears.

The other pirates and their captain, I had seen before; they had inhabited the island on and off for years. But Smee was something new. I listened to the cobwebs of his memory. A human might think memories are fainter than present thoughts, but that is not the case. Often, they are easy paths to follow for a faerie, and sometimes they are so loud they drown out everything else in the brain.

Smee had killed his first man at the age of twelve. The product of a privileged and sheltered life, he found the difficulty of murder had appealed to him: he loved doing something so frightening. It wasn't that Reginald was heartless. Quite the opposite. He sympathized with his victims, wondered about who they would leave behind. He felt deeply the despair of the man's or woman's final moments. He never killed without having to wipe a tear or two from his eyes, and that was how Tiger Lily had found him crying, after they'd pushed the pleading, terrified Englishman off the cliffs. It wasn't that he didn't care. I listened on, and shivered down to my little faerie bones. Reginald didn't kill because he had no heart. He killed because he did. He killed to make himself cry, and he only killed the people he admired.

By the time he was sixteen, the trail of violence he'd left

was being called a "rash of murders." In the papers, he was named "the South Bank Strangler." Reginald walked through the streets during those days, waiting for someone to point the finger. But no one looked at him, except to say "excuse me, sir" if they bumped into him.

This was in the time when spice was no longer king, when ships were crowding the ports with loads of cotton instead of cinnamon. People sat in parlors and talked about the unknowns. And there were so many. Where would expansion end? What was left to be invented? If there had been one symbol to define the minds and hearts of London at that time, it would have been a question mark. Smec had often gravitated to the docks, this question mark pushing him there.

That was where the captain found him. I don't know how he managed to single him out, or how he managed to be the only person in London who guessed that Reginald and the South Bank Strangler were one and the same.

To Reginald, the captain appeared at first to be an outline in the fog, in a long wig. He looked about as wealthy and refined an English gentleman as Reginald himself. But something made Reginald shiver at the sight of him— perhaps it was that the frills at his throat appeared to be out of place, old and slightly frayed, and his shirtsleeves seemed to be twilling apart at the cuffs, and then, beneath the cuffs, something was uneven, and Reginald finally understood what it was: the missing hand.

There were no pirates anymore. Not like this one—arrayed in Louis XVI garb and with a wig like a barrister, only powdered black with coal. The loss of his hand was recent, the wound crisscrossed with thick, black, crooked stitches. Up close, there was nothing refined about him at all. The many lines in his face were caked with dirt, his lips were crusty, and his flat blue eyes were bloodshot but friendly. He stank of cheap tobacco and whiskey, and clutched a cup of it in his left hand. He looked broken, and deadly.

He said, "Reginald Smee, I can see you're a born hunter. So I am requesting the pleasure of your company elsewhere." Then he grasped him around the arm and pulled him forward. He waved the stump at Smee. "Come now. No time to hesitate. We have hunting to do."

"W-what do you hunt, sir?" Reginald asked.

"Not sir. Just Hook." The stranger smiled, friendly. "I used to hunt ships. But recently I've switched. Now I hunt boys." He clapped Reginald on the back. "Now we both do."

It had been a rude awakening for Smee to leave England with a promise of paradise, and to end up in the thick, insect-infested, dirty, hot danger of the jungle. And while he'd been treated to a few amazing sights of creatures different from any in England—clusters of white-lit faeries hovering over a bog, furry beasts with tusks and horns—Neverland was mostly a tangle: of trees, of weeds, of predators, of quick deaths. Not to mention he was now bound to a man turning yellow from drink, not one-tenth so polished as he'd appeared on the docks of London, and half crazy.

The fact was, the captain was two men: one when he was sober, and one when he wasn't. Sober, Hook was charming, erudite, well-read, sharp, well-spoken, and thoughtful. Hook would be the first one to notice your water was empty, or that you needed another helping on your plate, or to make you feel like his favorite and most honored guest. Drunk, Hook was angry and sloppy. His eyes turned red and glassy almost as soon as spirits touched his lips. He went from rational to illogical, and most of all enraged. It was not hard to imagine that he had once been terrifying. He could still be scary, murderous in fact, but he was a broken man.

Still, a strong desire to please the captain, and be loved by him, was evident in all of the men around him, and Smee was turning out to be no exception. As they ate, he kept a solicitous eye on the captain's cup, and filled it each time it ran out. He, like the others, laughed loudly at the captain's jokes, making him smile with smug satisfaction. I guess it was Hook's rare combination of charm and utter intimidation that won not just fear from the crew, but love. Everyone clearly longed to be the captain's favored man, partly because it was such a difficult position to hold on to for long. And it was obvious that Smee was currently it. In the moonlight, the captain threw his arm around him from time to time, as he talked about his favorite drunken subjects—his missing hand, and the lost boys.

Sometimes he wore the hook from which he'd gotten his nickname, to substitute for his missing hand so that it was easier for him to grab things, and sometimes he didn't. It rarely stayed in place, and seemed to chafe and irritate him. He said he liked how it made him look but that it often rendered him more clumsy. Most of the men, he confided, believed he'd lost his hand in a fight, and that it had fallen into the ocean and been eaten by a crocodile.

"But," he confessed to Smee, "it came off in an assembly line." He gazed into Smee's eyes unsteadily. Smee knew he would never admit this while sober. "I worked on shoes, you see, to pay for school. It was my job to insert the leather into the machine, to be cut into the shape of the sole. You see?" He moved his hands in the air to imitate how he had done his work; then he stopped short and leaned forward with his elbows resting on his knees, his eyes glistening and red. "I was staying up nights to study. I thought I could study my way into being a gentleman. Well, I fell asleep. My hand went in instead of the leather." He grinned, almost as if it were a good joke. "You can see that the cut's shaped like a heel." He held up his rounded stump. His eyes seemed to focus. Then he quickly looped his arm around Smee's neck. Smee felt his breath on his cheek, steady and fast. "You tell anyone, I'll kill you."

Smee nodded. Hook licked his lips and sat back, relaxed again. "They think Peter chopped it off. Never. I *named* the lost boys, you know. I lost one, two, three of them. I started asking around, to all the tribes. 'Have you seen my lost boys?' And the name stuck."

Hook's fingers always twitched when he spoke of Pan. It turned him dark and antsy, and his jaw clenched and unclenched. It was an old grudge, and Smee still didn't understand where it had begun. All he knew was that Hook was stuck on it: he sometimes repeated a conversation over and over again, that he imagined he was having with Peter.

"Now that I have you, we'll have them," Hook said, and clapped Smee on the back. "You and I are thinkers. It's our minds that will allow us to thrive at what we do." Hook smiled. He was in a glowing mood after flinging the Englander into the sea. "We know he's in the area. He rescued the girl. Or took her to kill her. Not sure."

"I wouldn't mind strangling that girl myself." Smee stroked his cheek wound, almost lovingly.

Hook frowned. "Out of the question. I can't have trouble from the Sky Eaters. We have a truce. Don't touch her. Ever."

When Smee was silent, Hook turned a searching, piercing look on him. And it sent visible chills through Smee. But I was the one who could see how deeply Tiger Lily had affected Smee. A brave, strong girl; a powerful creature; a hunter. And though her looks were striking, they weren't what he was thinking of, but her big, wild, beating heart. She had held him in her hands, and spared him. What a magnificent creature. He would have to kill her.

I could see that even the threat of the captain's gaze couldn't dissuade him from the idea that he'd have to find the girl when she was unprotected, and strike.

It was Pan that Hook wanted, not Tiger Lily. But I knew, from a long night of listening, that Reginald Smee simply wouldn't be able to help himself.

ELEVEN

"I depart as air, I shake my white locks at the runaway sun,
"I effuse my flesh in eddies, and drift it in lacy jags.

"I bequeath myself to the dirt to grow from the grass I love,
"If you want me again look for me under your boot-soles."

P ine Sap leaned over Tik Tok's book in deep concentration. Pine Sap was one of the few villagers who had learned to read, from Tik Tok, who'd learned from a Bog Dweller who'd learned from a pirate over a hundred years before. Pine Sap, who had a knack for mental challenges and puzzles, had taken to it with ease.

Outside, the forest was deafening with rain, and about nine of the women, plus Pine Sap, were gathered in a drying hut staying warm and out of the wet. The rains had set in so that the days were waterlogged and the tribe had to take to shelter and entertain themselves. This was often done through singing and storytelling. Now Pine Sap, left out of a game the boys were having, was doing it with a book.

"What is he talking about?" Tiger Lily asked.

"Dying," Pine Sap said. "He's saying we live forever, but in different forms."

Tiger Lily's forehead bunched together in a crease. She didn't understand these things that Pine Sap seemed to get so easily. It frustrated her. And she didn't see the point of his obsession with knowing and reading and thinking.

Some of the women occasionally leaned over and rubbed his head, or patted his arm, and he squirmed and smiled politely and tried to move a bit farther away. The women liked to pamper and fuss over Pine Sap. Their maternal hearts were unable to resist his crookedness, his thin arms, the dimple under his squintier eye. He hated it. It was inexplicable that he braved the whole group of them on days like this.

Usually, Tik Tok would have been here too, among the women, but he liked to use the rain as an opportunity to make a special salve for his hair, to keep it shining and soft. Across a log he had left the beginning of Tiger Lily's wedding dress, which he'd pieced together from an exquisite suede he'd cured over several long days, skinning the deer himself—as all tribespeople knew how to do—boiling its hooves for a paste to help remove the fur, pulverizing its brains, and rubbing them on to soften the leather before hanging it over a fire for hours. He'd begun an intricate pattern of beadwork that would take several more months to finish. Like everything he did, the dress was being patiently and intricately constructed.

Moon Eye was curled against the wall next to Pine Sap, her knees pulled up to her chin, her long limbs prominent and folded around her like a dead spider's. She seemed to be growing longer all the time—twig thin, her legs didn't carry her forward these days; she just unwound in each direction she walked. She was another one who had taken up reading easily, and she peered over Pine Sap's shoulder, entranced. The women sat focused on their work, Aunt Agda and Aunt Sticky Feet, a woman named Bat Wing and the younger women, shaking their heads at the words of the poem to show it mystified them. Only Moon Eye seemed moved. But in her quiet, meek way, she kept silent.

"I've heard a lot of poetry now, and I've decided I don't like it," Tiger Lily said impulsively. Truly, it made her feel foolish, but she didn't say that.

"You're always so impatient," Pine Sap said.

Tiger Lily closed her lips hard and looked down at her work. And Pine Sap clearly realized he'd hurt her feelings, and regretted it. Pine Sap was one of the few people who could recognize what hurt feelings looked like on Tiger Lily's smooth, closed face.

A fog had come down on Neverland, and the path to Giant's was filled with it. The rain would come by midday. Now that the rainy season had arrived, it would be relentless.

Moon Eye fell in step with Tiger Lily as she walked to

Giant's house. "I'll come help you," she said.

"Don't," Tiger Lily said quietly. But Moon Eye silently followed along anyway.

Giant was sleeping when they got there. I flew up into the rafters to get out of the way of his smell. He reeked of clove oil, which, from the look of his glistening, enormous bare chest, he'd rubbed all over himself before bed.

He woke with a start, and stood slowly. He seemed even bigger indoors. His head looked heavy on his body. He had the dull face of someone who thought little. He sat down to let Tiger Lily brush his hair.

Whatever lice didn't live in the forest had apparently migrated to Giant's head. Tiger Lily stood behind him, combing the little bugs out one by one, expressionless.

Everyone whispered it wasn't wise for him to incur the wrath of the crows. But, perhaps because of his size, Giant was oblivious to all sorts of fear, including a fear of pushing Tiger Lily too hard. That was why he made her come to brush his hair every day, and why he left his house as messy as possible, for her to clean. He didn't have the audacity yet to touch her, and in all truth, it was obvious to everyone that she wasn't his type—that from the way he watched Moon Eye, he liked girls small and delicate. Still, he would very clearly have the audacity when they were married. This was the only reaction Tiger Lily showed to any of it: that when Giant stared at Moon Eye, a lustful smile on his half-open lips, Tiger Lily protectively stepped in front of her to block his view.

Aunt Fire soon appeared, as she was never far from her son. She lounged across a pillow on the floor, sucking on a chicken bone and occasionally pointing out bugs Tiger Lily had missed.

Since the day the pirates had disposed of Phillip, Tiger Lily was like a hide scraped bare. She berated herself for failing to protect him.

There was a hollow sound wherever she went. Pine Sap was always there trying to fill it with himself, hovering five steps behind her. Perhaps it was because of him that Moon Eye hovered too. The two followed her about like twins, and seemed to grow a regard for each other, but their concern made her feel smothered.

She tried to throw them off her trail. She ducked out of their sight after dinners. She left things for Pine Sap to trip on. She rigged a trap near her door that poured dirty, used laundry water on him twice. I worried for his feelings, and felt mortified by Tiger Lily's mean-spiritedness. But I didn't need to. Pine Sap was undeterred.

After she'd finished at Giant's, she walked to Tik Tok's house and sat to sew with him. Some of the women came there sometimes to get away from the wet weather.

Beside her, he worked with limitless patience, often stopping to help others with their work. Tiger Lily kept pricking her own fingers.

"You are cruel to Pine Sap," he said.

"He smothers me," she said.

"He's trying to be what you need."

"Constantly." She scowled at her work.

"Having someone who is constant isn't such a bad thing. In fact, it can be rare."

A thought of Pan flashed through Tiger Lily's mind, but she kept silent. She worried that if she mentioned him, she'd never be allowed into the woods again.

Tik Tok put down his work and stretched. He pulled his clock down off of his shelf and wound it thoughtfully.

"I'm not myself," she offered, guilty. She softened around Tik Tok, and when she did she was, for those rare moments, girlish.

He smiled. "You can never say that. You're just a piece of yourself right now that you don't like."

Afterward, chastened, she sought out Pine Sap and Moon Eye near a boulder by the river, lost in the book she'd brought back.

"I'm sorry I'm not a nicer person," she said, to both of them.

"It's all right," Moon Eye said in a voice thin as a reed; she played demurely with the flowers in her hands, which she was weaving into garlands for her mother. Pine Sap smiled with pleasure, and playfully poked at the crow feather in Tiger Lily's hair.

"Don't worry about it," he said.

Aunt Fire appeared behind her. "I need you," she barked.

"Giant has a boil on his big toe you need to lance."

Pine Sap winced. Moon Eye turned pale at the thought of Giant's feet. But Tiger Lily showed nothing but indifference, and turned and followed her future mother-in-law to her fate.

In the days that followed, I often wondered if Tiger Lily thought about Pan like I did. Sometimes her mind was foggy to me.

Was he a boy? A ghost? A cannibal? How many people had he killed? Would she ever try to go back and retrieve her necklace? And if so, how would she find him?

But Tiger Lily didn't have to track her way back to Peter Pan. Four days later, she was invited.

TWELVE

It was a piece of paper on her bed, when she walked in
after dinner.

On it was a map, but one only Tiger Lily could
understand, because it began at the tree where Pan had held
her captive.

It said two simple words: *Find us.*

For the next several days, she debated whether to go or
not. Most likely, it was a trap. The lost boys were known to
be vicious and cunning. But I knew Tiger Lily, and I knew
her curiosity would win out.

Tiger Lily's house was on the edge of the village, more in
the woods than not. And the village was large, and scattered.
Some people spent the day at the river, fishing. Some hunted
in the low brush that bordered the woods. Some worked in

drying huts and some worked in the dusty fields far to the west of the main square. Aside from Aunt Fire, no one would notice her absence. And this morning, Aunt Fire was busy in the manioc fields.

Tiger Lily slipped into the woods and left the village behind. She tracked landmarks she'd noted even when running from Pan. The leaves had been smoothed back over the spot where she'd been tied, but she bent to smell the mud.

From here, she followed his tracks, only consulting the map rarely. All but the most trained eye would have passed over the subtle signs: a rip in a leaf, an inch-long indent in the dirt. Even Tiger Lily's eyes failed in some places, a rarity. It was clear Pan and whoever else had taken great care to hide themselves. The tracks led deeper and deeper into the forbidden territory.

Soon, the number of these signs picked up, to show a commonly trodden area, touched by many sets of feet.

These footprints led into a deep trench that would have been easy to walk by without noticing at all, even for a tracker. Here she became confused. There was a tree stump rooted into the ground, and tracks scuttled around it, but the trench ended, gradually rising back to ground level.

She heard the vaguest rumble of something underneath her. It was barely a whisper. She looked at the stump. Its roots were all exposed.

Uncertainly, she pulled at the stump, and let out a gasp

when it came loose easily. She pulled harder, tilting it onto its side.

She was peering into a dark hole. Tiger Lily stood, looking around the empty woods for signs of someone watching her. But the woods were eerily quiet.

After a moment's hesitation, she lowered herself inside in one fluid, silent movement. I followed just behind her. The entry dropped us into a wide, dimly lit, earth-walled tunnel, where Tiger Lily landed with her dagger drawn, keeping her back to the low dirt wall.

The place was filled with skulls—skulls hanging from the roots jutting from the dirt above us, identified by badly spelled pirate names, like Crucked Tow and Baldy, painted on pieces of bark.

The cave narrowed into a small doorway, then opened out into a wide room, lit by a few candles melted onto rocks.

In this room, in various states of disarray, figures lay curled in heaps. They were under blankets or not, some with legs splayed, some crooked and curled up, all asleep. There were empty bottles littering the floor and a clay pot had been knocked over and broken—it looked like they'd been celebrating something. Snores abbreviated the silence.

But for one figure, they were all lying directly on the dirt. There was one comfortable spot, a mattress of hay flush against a wall, and there Pan slept, curled onto his side, the pearl dangling from his neck. The others spiraled out around him in piles as if guarding him in sleep. Up ahead of her, I was already at Pan's face, and could see the three thin long lines of finger-shaped bruises Tiger Lily had left on his neck. She picked her way across the sleeping bodies, held the necklace gently away from his chest, and lifted her knife to slice it from him, his breath landing against her wrists. In sleep, he had a strangely beautiful face.

When I looked up, his eyes were open, and he was staring at me. I saw a moment before she did.

His arm moved fast as a viper, and she jerked, but it was too fast and he had her by her braid. He smiled.

The bodies began to stir.

Peter scurried down beside her, squatting. I don't know how he moved so quickly.

"You're here," he said. And let go of her. The boys were wide-awake now, crowding toward her. One boy held half of the clay pot poised in the air, ready to hit her. They all looked to be about Pan's age, maybe fifteen or sixteen, lanky for the most part, muscularly and yet awkwardly built.

"Here." Pan reached up to his neck and held out the necklace. "You want this." He untied it, and handed it to her. The boys, deflating, lowered their arms, but still stood on the alert and looked at Pan for his next move.

He was silent for several moments, his hair crooked from sleep, his face soft and vulnerable because he wasn't yet fully awake. Finally, he cleared his throat. "I never introduced myself. I'm Peter." He looked around at the others, and his mouth tilted in a rueful, ironic smile. "We've never had a girl here. We're in bad shape. I'm sorry. Thank you for coming."

Tiger Lily looked around at them. As she turned, one of the boys ducked up behind her and rubbed his hand along her braid.

She startled.

"Sorry," he said.

"She'll tell someone," a burly boy said. "We should kill her."

Peter kept his eyes on Tiger Lily as he replied, "She won't tell anyone."

"She probably knows the pirates," the boy said.

"She hates pirates. I caught her trying to kill one."

"Still I don't see why we should change everything now, just because . . ." Suddenly, he got quiet. Peter was giving him a look that shut him up.

Peter turned and stared at Tiger Lily awkwardly for a moment, and there was a heavy, uncomfortable silence. Then another boy stepped forward and held out his hand. When she only stared at it, he took her hand in his. He was a well-proportioned boy, with sloppy, wavy brown hair and an open, confident face. He had the twinkly-eyed look of someone who'd never been nervous or self-doubtful a day in his life. "I'm Nibs. The one who tried to molest your hair is Tootles." The boy called Tootles looked abashed. He was skinny and frail, like he'd grown too fast for his skeleton to catch up. He seemed to be stretched out like taffy, with big grayish circles around his eyes, pale cheeks, all shoulders that hunched to compensate for his height, and a timid air. "And we wouldn't kill you. I mean, maybe Slightly would, but he's a monster." He gestured toward the burly boy who'd spoken earlier—despite his name, Slightly was anything but slight. Hefty, solid, with a wooden whistle hanging around his neck, he was just a bit shorter than Tiger Lily, but filled out and the most adult looking of all of them.

"Is he really a girl?" Slightly asked. Peter hit him hard in the bicep, then looked at Tiger Lily, embarrassed.

"Ignore him," Nibs said. "He's cranky because he didn't get enough sleep. Plus he thinks he remembers England, and it makes him annoying. I'm sure many people would say you're a prettyish girl." He leaned his hand on the shoulder of a boy with long, straight hair. "This is Curly. Watch him. He's practically diabolical. Just because he's quiet doesn't mean he's nice." Curly stared at her with half-crazed green eyes and a mischievous smile.

"I don't see why, if a girl was going to visit, she couldn't be a girl with some curves," Slightly said, and this time Nibs hit him. Slightly got a mock-offended look on his face and pointed to Tootles. "*He* said it!"

Tootles clearly hadn't said it, and upon being accused, he just looked depressed. He let out a sigh. "Leave me out of it," he muttered.

Tiger Lily took it all in silently. These were the lost boys. They didn't look like killers. They looked like disheveled and half-starved teenage boys.

"Those over there"—Nibs nodded at two identical boys standing by a wooden mermaid clearly pilfered or scavenged from a ship, whispering to each other—"are the twins." He dropped his voice to a murmur. "We never know which is which. Don't bother trying to figure it out. One of them said it makes him feel like he doesn't have an identity. Couldn't be bothered telling which one it was."

The twins scowled at him, and one pretended to laugh and then went suddenly serious-faced.

"Stay the afternoon," Peter said, interrupting impatiently.

As they all stood staring at each other, Peter shifted from one foot to the other restlessly, as if the whole thing was too buttoned down and agonizing for him, and he couldn't wait for it to be over. He looked only at her. She stood rodlike next to the litheness of him. Curly was the only one who seemed to notice me, and he reached up to try to swat me. I circled back and bit him on the shoulder, then perched up in a depression of rock and glared at him.

Peter seemed to cast about for something to say. "Do you want to see the place?" he asked. Tiger Lily considered. She had what she'd come for, and now the smart thing would be to leave. She had never seen any creatures quite like the lost boys, and it was possible they were more dangerous than she thought. But Peter walked, and without really choosing to, she followed. I watched Tiger Lily's eyes drift to the bruises she'd left on Peter's neck. But if he remembered them, he didn't let on.

The boys did indeed look underfed. But the hunger with which they gazed at Tiger Lily was something different. It was like a desperate need to be near someone new.

"We've built it all from scratch," Peter threw over his shoulder. Behind him, Tootles bumped his head on the ceiling and winced, glancing back at her, embarrassed. Curly snorted. "When we built this place, we never thought we'd get so tall," Peter said. "I didn't think ahead," he said sheepishly. Nibs patted him on the back as if to say he was being too hard on himself.

The long narrow hall they'd entered gave way to a door that had been left unlatched, and which opened onto an ingeniously finished network of rooms. The floors had been covered with rough wooden planks; the walls had been carved straight and even dotted with nails, from which hung decorations: pieces of braided rope, elaborate animal skulls, shells. Also knives, arrows, a couple of swords, ropes, and loose spikes.

The years of intricate work and artistry that must have gone into the rooms contrasted with the crude weapons, and especially with the boys' slovenly appearance. They were all dressed in clothes that were too small and falling apart. They clearly hadn't bathed in weeks. Admittedly, the place was also a mess. Mummified apple cores. Blankets strewn everywhere. Clothes dropped where they'd been taken off. It had a thick masculine smell that was part dirt and part something deeper. Some things looked to be sitting in the same places they'd been left years ago.

"We made a room just for belly fighting," Nibs said, "and rolling down an incline in our blankets, but we're over that, obviously."

Peter looked embarrassed, so he went on to qualify his words: "We're too old." As if he had to explain.

"Especially Tootles," one of the twins said.

"I'm the same age as you," Tootles muttered, but no one paid attention. Nibs gave Tootles an affectionate rub on top of his head.

"Ignore them, buddy."

There was a joyfulness and—at the same time—a fragility about each of them. They were sloppy and uncared for and wildly alert and full of energy. Though they looked to be about the same age as some of the teenage warriors of Tiger Lily's tribe, they moved and spoke like they were of a different species altogether. In her tribe, the boys were very determined to act like men. They stood straight, didn't talk much to girls, and followed a strict code. These boys were more like animals than boys, even in the way they pushed and muttered at each other as they moved in a gaggle behind Peter. There were weapons perched in nooks and crannies—some of the blades with old browned bloodstains—next to decks of cards, dreamy drawings in charcoal, and little exquisite but half-finished carvings of beasts and faeries. Straw beds had been separated haphazardly into different areas of the burrow, as if the boys hadn't counted on wanting to live separately when they'd first built it, and only recently pushed themselves as far apart from each other as possible. Still, on one of the beds there was a worn home-sewn toy in the shape of a rabbit, and lying on a pillow, as if it had just been played with, a model of a ship.

Peter moved as if he couldn't get to each place quickly enough. He chopped his words off at the last consonant, as if it took too long to get the whole word out. And he had a habit of rubbing his index and middle finger back and forth across his bottom lip, which constantly drew my attention there and made me slightly giddy. The others clearly felt it too, because as they walked he was completely surrounded—the boys gravitated wherever he moved. He let out several loud rough laughs at their jokes, then turned to Tiger Lily to see if she was upset by the laughter.

I had heard rumors all my life that the lost boys could fly, and that they kept and tortured prisoners, but so far, I saw no evidence of either. They kept their feet on the ground, and they seemed only too happy to show every corner of the burrow, which looked to be prisonerless.

In the room where, Nibs explained, they prepared their meals, we suddenly came upon a baby, just lying on a lump of blankets in a trough.

"Oh"—Nibs's eyes widened—"I forgot. Sorry, Baby." He picked up the baby, then held it out to Tiger Lily. "This is Baby. Our baby. It seemed too much of a commitment to name him anything else."

He reached toward her, and Tiger Lily immediately crossed her arms to avoid having the bundle put into her hands. She was terrified of holding babies. She didn't like the way they squirmed, like holding a worm.

"Why do you have a baby?" she asked. Her voice was almost as low and deep as the boys'.

"She speaks," one of the twins said to the other.

"Peter found him after a pirate raid," Nibs said. "He's softhearted. Couldn't let him starve to death. We love him, but it's hard. Sometimes we forget him someplace and have to go back for him. Curly loves to dress him up. Today he's supposed to be a maggot." I had run into my share of maggots burrowing through rotten logs. Other than wearing brown, the baby looked nothing like a maggot, but Curly grinned with pride.

Suddenly, while Tiger Lily was unguarded, Nibs thrust Baby into her arms. He squirmed, blinked up at her sleepily, then began to scream. The boys all watched, waiting for her to do something, but she stood stiff. "Don't cry," she said finally, holding the baby out at arm's length. "Don't cry, Baby." Her words only seemed to make him scream louder. Finally, Tiger Lily lunged toward the trough and put the baby back into it and backed away, trying to pretend like he didn't exist. One of the twins appeared with a bottle and leaned over him, and soon he was quiet.

Pan didn't seem to notice any of it—he was studying a hangnail on his thumb and chewing on it. Finally he looked

81

up and walked on, in his half-graceful, half-ungainly walk, and we came to his room.

It was separate from the others, with a piece of cloth over the entranceway and candles stuck into nooks in the walls. It was stuffed with things he'd obviously collected. Drawings. Feathers and shells. Another half carving of a mermaid that looked like it had come from the stern of one of the Englanders' ships. Beside his bedroll, a little clay hand-fashioned cup. Scratchy spun blankets were piled at one corner. A flute. And lots of tiny carvings lying all over the place, whittled out of wood. They were all of birds. There must have been thirty or forty of them, but none quite done.

"I hate sitting still. I can't sit still long enough to come close to finishing anything." He looked around the room self-consciously. "The boys want to sleep here too, but I can't stand anyone sleeping next to me. It makes me itch," he said.

I flitted over to a carving of a seagull, and rested against its wing.

A book of some sort, perhaps stolen from the stone house, sat in a place of honor on a rough-hewn bench by the door as a decoration.

"Where are your families?" Tiger Lily asked.

Peter smiled, ran a hand through his bed-smushed hair so that it spiked to the left, then shrugged and slouched. "We don't have them. We don't want them."

Tiger Lily studied him evenly. He was a mystery to both of

us. His thoughts were still a dark jumble, and I had a feeling they were always that way, even when he felt peaceful. "Where did you come from?" she asked.

"Some of the boys were brought from England," Peter said, and a shadow came and went across his pale face as he looked over at Slightly. Then he brightened. "My parents died in a sinking and I floated to shore on a luggage trunk. Nibs and I have been here for years." He seemed to remember something, and disappeared from the room.

"We hide from the pirates here," Slightly said, speaking low, clearly so that Peter wouldn't hear.

"If they found us," Tootles murmured, "we'd all be dead."

Slightly thwacked him on the shoulder, and Tootles winced.

"They hate us," one of the twins said. "They want us exterminated."

I heard now the fear in their brightness. It trickled along underneath them like a secret spring.

They all got quiet. Tiger Lily wondered why the pirates hated them, but didn't find her voice to ask. Then Peter returned and they all brightened. Curly's eyes drifted to me, and I could tell that he was never happy unless he was fiddling with something or smushing something or breaking something. Nibs reached up and touched the feather in Tiger's Lily hair. She jerked away.

"Did you find that feather yourself?" Nibs asked, undeterred. She nodded.

"You should keep it." He smiled. "It suits you." She softened.

"You have hairy arms," Tootles said. "Girls aren't supposed to."

"She's hairier than you," Slightly said to Tootles.

A blush ran across Tiger Lily's face, though she kept her gaze even. She thought of the photos of the English ladies she'd seen, smooth and white, and for a moment, it made her sad.

"Quiet!" Peter said, glancing at her expression. The boys looked abashed. "Get out of here. Go find something to do." The boys shuffled off forlornly. "I'm sorry," Peter said, his shoulders slumped self-consciously. "Don't leave. They don't know any girls. That's why I invited you."

"I don't care what they say," she said, though she did care.

"I think your arms are lovely, Tiger Lily," Nibs said loudly over his shoulder on his way out, making it worse.

"I have to go," she said. Through a tiny smoke hole in the room, she could see that the sky was darkening with the afternoon rain on the way. And she had what she'd come for. And she was still alive. She didn't know why she felt suddenly sad.

Peter looked regretful. He peered around the room, seemed to be thinking of how he could change her mind. But finally he said, "I'll walk you."

I considered trying to regurgitate that morning's gnat breakfast on Curly's head before we left, but I followed Peter and Tiger Lily out without incident. Peter walked her all the way to an old bridge, about half a mile from the burrow. Flying behind them, I could smell the same scent from Peter that had been in his room, musky, leafy, and boyish. As the two walked ahead of me, there was a rustle above us and one of the twins came rappelling down a tree. For the first time, I noticed ropes hidden up among the limbs, woven carefully through the lushest areas of leaves. Tiger Lily gasped. This, I realized, was how they had spread the rumor that they could fly. It was an elaborate network of ladders and tightropes that they probably retreated to when they didn't want to leave tracks. And it had all been hidden so well that I hadn't noticed. "Good-bye, native girl," the twin said. "It was nice to see you."

Then he turned and hurried back toward the burrow.

The bridge had been hand built, probably before any of them had been born. It was half rotten, and spanned a swampy trickle that came off the lagoon. Several crocodiles lay below, their mouths open and waiting. Peter chewed on his nails.

"They're always here because the boys like to feed them. They think I don't know. But it entertains them. One of the twins once threw a rat in for them, but I had to put an end to that."

"Why?" she asked.

He turned his lashy blue eyes on her; he had the kind of

open, disarming gaze that could make people lose their trains of thought, even boys. "Because it's not fair to the rat. You have to at least have a fighting chance."

Tiger Lily took this in silently. I watched the two of them. I liked the way they stood together. They both kept one ear on each other, and one on the forest around them. And yet, there was something almost peaceful about them standing there. Maybe the way he seemed to vibrate made her stillness seem less glaring, and Peter seemed calmer.

"You don't say much?" Peter said.

Tiger Lily shook her head. She was unsure what to say without revealing too much of herself.

Peter leaned on the railing, which was merely a long crooked stick suspended by two wooden forks. He swayed forward and back against it listlessly, pumping his arms slowly, looking for something else to say. The railing didn't appear to be sturdy enough to hold his weight for long. There were still parts of him that hadn't caught up to the rest of him. "We *do* know girls. It's not like we've never seen a girl. I love girls. I mean, I have loved a lot of them and there are some I love now. We know lots of girls actually." He leaned in, paused. "They say a lot more than you do. It's nice when they laugh."

Tiger Lily merely stared down at the water below, trying to absorb all of the information. Then suddenly, in a heartbeat, Peter's eyes turned to me, as if he'd been noticing me all along. He reached out and lifted his hand gently underneath me, studying me. Imagine a human touching a fly this way. Most humans don't find faeries worth studying and, if they do try to touch them, accidentally smush them or at least break a limb or two. But Peter touched me so carefully and gently that it felt like a whisper. "You're a pretty little thing," he said. Then, just as quickly, he set me onto a leaf and turned his attention back to Tiger Lily. He pointed across the thin swath of swamp to a tree just out of reach. A strange ball, trailing ribbons in a kind of tail, perched in the branches.

"Nibs made that ball for us when we were kids," he said. "You can twirl it and fling it really high. Too high, I guess. Slightly lost it there ages ago. No one can get it." He nodded down to the crocs. "I don't know why we'd want to get it anyway. We wouldn't play with it anymore. We've outgrown that kind of stuff. But still, Tootles wants it back in the worst way. Maybe it's for the memories."

Before he could say more, Tiger Lily was on the trunk of the tree, shinnying her way up. She moved like an eel, wriggling and quick, her strong legs carrying her higher and higher, until she was at the limb. I perched on the railing to watch and held my breath. Peter held his.

Ask a Bog Dweller about endurance. But for things requiring balance and strategy, Sky Eaters were the most graceful and accomplished people in all of Neverland. Even faeries marveled at their skill. And Tiger Lily was easily their best climber. Here was an impossibly skinny limb, but she distributed her weight expertly. And simply, so quickly that it seemed without thought or effort, she had the ball in her hands, its ribbons still wrapped in twigs and thick leaves.

She climbed down and gave the ball to Peter.

"Thank you for giving me my necklace back," she said, with a great effort.

Peter stared at the ball in his hand and frowned. Then he looked at her as if he felt sorry for her. "We could have done that. But the hard part is unraveling the ribbons from the leaves, that's what I meant. It's just a pain. That's all."

She tilted her head, confused. "Oh," she said.

"You looked strange climbing in the tree like that."

Tiger Lily pulled her braids between her fingers, her sudden self-consciousness feeling foreign and strange to her. "I didn't do it to look nice," she said.

"But you do care."

Tiger Lily studied the tree and decided if she did care, she would now choose not to. "I don't," she said.

"All girls do," he added, pushing the point.

"You must not know many girls."

"I know a million," Peter said, dark and serious. There was a long awkward silence, but if Peter regretted his words, I couldn't tell.

"Did you cry? About your friend?" he finally asked, changing the subject.

She shook her head. She couldn't have cried if she wanted to. Other girls in her village cried a lot. Boys claimed not to cry, but she had seen Pine Sap cry harder than anyone, over a wounded bird. Then again, he had a special connection to birds. Learned all their calls. Knew their habits.

"Yeah." Peter picked at his hangnail again. "Actually, I never get sad. It's a waste of time, don't you think?"

Tiger Lily didn't answer. She was impressed by the idea of deciding not to be sad. His words made him seem very strong. Impervious.

"Why did you look after that man?" Peter asked.

Tiger Lily considered the question. "I didn't want him to be alone," she finally said.

Peter kept his eyes on her for a long while. She looked up at the moving gray clouds and resumed walking.

Peter followed her. We reached the edge of his territory. When she turned to say good-bye, his face was dark.

"You'll come back?"

She shook her head. I looked into the shade. When the clouds drifted in, the forest became dark a few feet away. "No. I'll never come back. I wouldn't be allowed."

Having had an eye on Tiger Lily since she was a child, I knew a few things. She had many flaws. Conceit. Stubbornness. Pride. But breaking her word wasn't one of them. I knew, when she said it, we would not be returning to Peter and the burrow.

Peter took this in. "Well, I wish it was different," he said sadly. He stopped short. He stuck out his hand, and she stared at it. "You shake it. Something Slightly taught us. It's polite."

He took her hand and moved it up and down to demonstrate. She let him, silently. He hung on to her fingers.

Suddenly he stepped forward and pulled her toward him and hugged her tightly. When he set her loose, she tottered.

"Okay, good-bye," he said. Then he turned, as if forgetting her, and walked toward the burrow without a backward glance. Me, he had already forgotten for sure. But I watched him walk away. I didn't know why, but I couldn't not. He had scooped me up. He had looked at me with his lashy eyes.

We were too late to get to the village before the rain. I dodged the drops, and I managed to stay dry, but by the time we got home, Tiger Lily was soaked. And me . . . I was fairly certain I was in love.

THIRTEEN

The second time the village decided Tiger Lily was cursed, it was when Aunt Fire burned herself alive.

Tiger Lily was sitting by the fire, listening to Pine Sap talk about the fascinating and mysterious traits of crows. He loved to study the ways birds lived and how they built their nests and the different, intricate ways they spoke to each other, and recently he'd become fixated on crows in particular . . . perhaps because he thought it might interest Tiger Lily, which it didn't. He was regaling her with a description of a crow funeral and the tribal behavior of groups of crows when Aunt Fire appeared, her saggy face red and pulled tightly down in rage over some chore that Tiger Lily had left undone in Giant's hut. She lifted the broom and beat Tiger Lily about the head and shoulders, knocking her bowl of corn and beans into the fire and sending Tiger Lily pitching forward.

Tiger Lily was physically strong. She could have snapped Aunt Fire in half like a twig. But she took the beating, lying down on the ground, too stubborn to even cover her head as the broom repeatedly struck her skull. All of Aunt Fire's rage at every insult she had ever received rained down in those blows.

Then, when her abuser had spent her limited energy, Tiger Lily simply stood up, and walked off toward her hut.

A few minutes later, Aunt Fire was leaning by the fire, talking to Aunt Sticky Feet about the filth in Giant's room, when she lost her balance, ever so slightly, and fell right onto the flames that happened to be cooking that day's lunch.

It was almost as if she'd been doused in oil, it caught so quickly. She went thrashing about, running through the village, calling for help. But the speed only fanned the flames. Before anyone could stop her, or jump on her with blankets, she was at the other edge of the village, a black, smoking nightmare of a creature. She collapsed, and suddenly went silent.

As it happened, a crow was eating an ear of corn on a log just beside where she collapsed. The crow had stolen the corn from the tribe's meal—so it had recently been roasted by the fire too.

When Tiger Lily came out of her house a few moments later, having missed the commotion completely, everyone turned to look at her.

After that day, Pine Sap disappeared into the woods every morning and came home every afternoon, and no one paid any attention. It seemed that he was distancing himself from Tiger Lily, at last. He wasn't terribly useful for any of the village tasks, and the boys were glad to be without him on their hunts, because he always slowed them down. I must confess that even I never followed him, for lack of curiosity. My thoughts were on Tiger Lily, as were everyone else's.

The village watched her out of the sides of their eyes. It oppressed her, and we all wondered what she would do. The only thing we wondered more was what *Giant* would do. And the hopeful among us, myself included, thought he would never marry his mother's suspected murderer.

For several days, Giant stayed away, mourning by himself across the river. When the tribe buried Aunt Fire on a hill overlooking the water—where all of the tribe's dead were laid to rest—he stayed away. Tik Tok presided over the ceremony in a solemn deep-green dress, and spoke about the continuity of the spirit.

It was during those days that Giant first came after Moon Eye, when she was down by the river washing her hair. She had come to sit at the water's edge, and he came upon her accidentally through the bushes. He startled her. Then he grabbed the edges of her dress. She pulled out of his grasp, and ran back to the council fire, where she lodged herself at Pine Sap's side and never said a word.

*   *   *

Everyone watched Tiger Lily's house for signs of contrition. Until she came out one night, and approached the fire where everyone was gathered for dinner. There was a collective holding of breath when they saw her, and only later did they whisper about what to make of it.

Nothing had changed about her, except that she was wearing two feathers in her hair instead of one.

I confess. I flew back to the burrow on secret, nightly visits. I watched Peter and the boys. I nestled behind Peter's ear one night while he slept. I lay on his chest and listened to him breathe. I wanted to be close to him and smell him and hear his heartbeat.

I watched the lost boys living without a girl in sight. I watched how they existed hand to mouth, from one kill to the next. And how they wondered what else there was out there to see and do and what was missing. Next to Tiger Lily, Peter was the loneliest person I'd ever set eyes on. But mostly, I saw something they wouldn't let anyone else see. How scared they were, and how well they hid. And I knew, too, what they hid from, and how much they should fear.

FOURTEEN

I believed she wouldn't go back until the moment she was walking into the woods, three days after the village buried Aunt Fire. Maybe it was the suffocation of everyone's stares that made her break her word. Or maybe, as I thought later, there was just something about the boys that drew her back.

It was a little before dusk, and she slipped away effortlessly, as almost no one dared come by her house now, and those who did would think she was down at the river, or over in the manioc fields. She made her way to the burrow easily enough, through the tangled, humid woods, over the crocs nipping at her from under the footbridge. I followed with slightly trembling wings.

The burrow was empty, but Tiger Lily followed the

footprints (in the shape of bears' tracks—they must have worn decoys on their feet) down to a lagoon. Tiger Lily wasn't fooled. I floated on a breeze in her wake.

The lagoon was tidal, with the giant, tree limb–filled dwelling of an enormous Never bird the only thing floating on its surface. This Never bird had probably taken years to build its huge nest—it measured about as wide as an average man was long, and was filled with all sorts of colorful feathers pilfered from other birds, as Never birds—much like birds all over the world—attract their mates with a show of how beautifully they can decorate. The water itself had a deep, briny, muddy smell, and cool air drifted off its surface. It reached like a fat thumb inland from the sea, where it lay still and muted and peaceful. From here, it was hard to guess that, just beyond the tilt and shelter of the hills that surrounded the lagoon on three sides, the ocean roared.

Tonight, the shore of the lagoon had been festooned with torches. Peter was there, with the others, perched by the water, watching its glossy surface. It was one of the twins who first spotted her, and let out a whoop.

"You're just in time," Nibs said breathlessly. "We're having a dance."

"A dance?" she asked uncertainly.

"It's an English thing. Except in England there are girls. We're honoring Tootles because it's his birthday. We think." He smiled sheepishly. "At least, that's what we've decided. We throw him a lot of parties to make up for all the other times we can't help making fun of him. I don't know if you've noticed he's an easy target." Tiger Lily had noticed.

Peter stood and smiled at her, rubbing his dirty hands on his thighs and then reaching out to shake hers, awkwardly. "You weren't coming back," he said. His mouth tilted up reluctantly, like a smile he was trying to keep in. She didn't answer, but let him grasp her fingers in his strange gesture of manners. He didn't seem to notice me.

They had all bathed, in their own way. They looked cleaner than they had the last time Tiger Lily had come, though still disheveled. Peter's hair was mushed to one side as before, but his pale skin was clean and glowing. He was beautiful, there was no way anyone could deny it.

There was an awkward silence, and Tiger Lily felt it. "What are you looking at?" she asked.

"There are jellyfish in the water," Peter said to her. "Here." He pulled her down beside him. "They can't survive in any other kind of water, just this lagoon. If they float too close to the surface, they die. They're here forever and nowhere else." He turned his big eyes to her solemnly. "They never can go see the ocean. It's tragic."

She looked down at the water. She could see the ghostly shapes of the jellyfish, but so deep she might have been imagining them.

While the others were absorbed in what was underwater, I scanned the surface of the water from one end of the lagoon to the other, out of habit. For years after my father left us for

97

Belladonna, I had looked for him . . . the last time someone had seen them, they were living on a duck's back. But I had never been able to find him. I no longer really thought I might. But scanning the waters was a habit.

"Well," Peter said after several minutes. "Should we start the dance?"

Tootles retrieved jars of a brown, fetid liquid from the burrow. In fact, Tootles seemed to run most of the errands for his own party. He hurried from here to there, jamming torches into the ground, before returning to the circle. They all—except Tiger Lily, who politely refused—began to drink from their jars.

I tried to make myself useful. I brought edible flowers to put in Peter's drink. I held a leaf and fanned his ear to keep him cool. He barely seemed to notice. I secretly spit in Curly's jar when he wasn't looking.

A mermaid beached herself on a rock in the middle of the lagoon to watch the festivities. She was bare and sludge-covered from the torso up, and her slippery lower body lay twitching on the muddy, stony surface. She was all curves and mud, sharp teeth and soft lips. Barnacles had grown on her shoulders, her elbows, and at the curve of her neck, but she was still a magnificent animal. Peter walked to the water and waved to her, just gently.

"Why is she watching us so intently?" Tiger Lily asked Tootles.

"Oh, that's Maeryn. She wants Peter to go swim with her.

He does from time to time."

"But they'd murder him." Mermaids were among the most treacherous predators in all of Neverland. They were known to lurk in bodies of water no bigger than puddles, waiting to drown hapless swimmers, though faeries have nothing to fear from them because we are too small and bitter for them to eat.

"No." Tootles shook his head. "The mermaids are in love with Peter. That one most of all."

"And Peter loves them," Slightly added cynically. "In his way."

Tiger Lily looked out at the mermaid. She thought of Peter underwater, with the darkness, the mud, the fish, and the hidden places. The things he would see that she likely never would.

"He can't even swim," Nibs said. "The mermaids have to do the paddling for him."

"Mermaids can't help being killers," Slightly said. "He shouldn't go in there."

"They can help it if it's Peter," Tootles said. "Everything goes his way."

Slightly rolled his eyes, but Nibs rubbed Tootles's head affectionately. He seemed to be the only one who sensed Tootles needed extra attention.

"We're lucky. He looks out for us." Nibs took a sip of his drink, and noticed Tiger Lily watching him curiously.

"We learned how to drink by spying on the Bog Dwellers.

We watched how they made beer. We were getting bored of everything else."

The mermaid made a splash as she slithered back into the water. I was glad. There was something menacing about the way she had sat watching.

The boys launched into the dance part of the night as best they could for a group of only boys. Curly played a long bamboo flute. The twins sang. I found a place to watch from a fern. They all became unrecognizable as the night went on. Tiger Lily sat like a statue, hands on her knees, back straight, out of her element. As they grew sloppier and less alert, the twins argued too loudly about whether Tiger Lily was ugly or beautiful, and finally agreed that she was "ugly beautiful." Tiger Lily pretended she hadn't heard, but her heart slowed to absorb the blow. Tootles and Nibs performed a small, spontaneous skit, and Slightly did a little ballet that made everyone laugh. Some of the boys played cricket with a skull for a while. Every time Tootles came to bat, he'd go running from base to base, holding his sagging pants up from behind, but not fast enough to keep half of his backside from being revealed in all its pale glory.

The more the boys drank, the more delinquent they became, Peter most of all. Curly put down his flute and started trying to light little things on fire. Peter showed them how to pull down a branch with his teeth, and chased Nibs into the trees and tackled him, making him scream, "Peter is the king and will live forever," before he'd let him up. Finally, Nibs took Tootles's hand and they slow-danced, each leaning against the other, like rag dolls. The twins soon did the same. It was proof of their loneliness for other people that they were willing to lean on each other so much, and Slightly played songs on Curly's flute that grew slower, more thoughtful, and melancholy.

I watched with a tugging feeling of sadness for them. I even had a passing longing for home. Faeries had dances too.

Nibs must have noticed that Tiger Lily was sitting alone, because abruptly he rose, made a direct line for her, and asked her to dance. They lumbered about. She stepped on his feet many times and barreled them both into a tree. It became a source of embarrassment—all eyes were on them— but Nibs courageously kept at it, clearly not wanting to desert her.

It was as quick as a blink: one minute she was falling into Nibs again, and the next she was caught squarely in front of Peter, his arms adjusting her so she'd dance steady, though it was the blind leading the blind, as Peter was no dancer either (he only seemed convinced he was). He lurched back and forth, correcting Tiger Lily with his hands.

"You just do this," he said. "It's easy."

Slightly, wobbly from drink, had started banging on a makeshift drum. "Don't you ever try to be quiet?" Tiger Lily asked Peter.

"Why would we?"

"To keep the beasts away."

"The bad things are some of my favorites," Peter said. Tiger Lily couldn't tell if he was a fool or only fearless. With most people, she would have thought the former. But it seemed possible that Peter wasn't scared of anything.

She looked around at the others, boys collapsed against each other in slow dances. "In our tribe, dancing is sacred," she said thoughtfully.

"Nothing here is sacred," Peter said. His mouth tilted to the left in a smile.

"That must be hard," she said. Peter frowned.

"Why did you come back?" he finally asked, changing the subject.

"I don't know," she said.

"It's been boring without you. Even though you only came that once." He tugged her close and seemed to hold on to her tight. Tiger Lily went stiff, and pulled back a bit, resembling a briar. Peter didn't seem to notice and kept firmly clasping her waist, but when the music ended, he let go of her hand without a thought. Later she found him surrounded by the boys, talking about a near escape from one of the pirates. They were all riveted, even though—she knew from the story—most of them had been there. Peter was animated, his cheeks flushed, a picture of both boyish excitement and a grown kind of toughness. He could have been talking about bananas, and the group would have been just as enrapt.

Sweaty and awake from the dancing, Tiger Lily stood with the others, arms crossed standoffishly, but included.

Finally you could tell—by the distinct quiet around the woods that came when the night animals had gone to sleep and the day animals were not yet awake, and the smell of buds and greenery just beginning to unfold for the morning sun—that it was the hour before dawn, and Tiger Lily knew she would have to get home.

The others, now half asleep and lying on the ground, listening to Slightly tell a story about roaches, didn't notice when she got up. She slipped off into the darkness without saying good-bye and, sitting in her collar, I saw him coming up behind her. For all his bragging, his confidence in this one talent was well-founded: I never saw anyone sneak up on Tiger Lily but Peter.

"I think we could be good friends," he said, falling into step with her. "It's perfect because I wouldn't fall in love with you, like I do with the mermaids. Girls always seem so exotic. But it would be okay with you, because you're more like . . . you know. Not like a girl." He shrugged. "Will you?"

"Will I?"

"Be friends." At that moment, I envied Tiger Lily for the first time.

"Here," he said, stopping her by holding her arm. He knelt before her. There were the same thin shoulder blades, like chicken wings. The thong of her shoe had come lose, and he tied it, and looked up at her while he did, causing her to hold her breath.

"When you come back, I can fix it permanently."

"I shouldn't come back," she said.

His mouth settled firmly in a frown. "But you'll be back. I know you will. You won't be able to let us go now."

FIFTEEN

A few days later, I was asleep down in her suede blanket when I heard her stir, and then leap. Beside her on her pillow was a gift from Giant: Aunt Fire's wedding bracelets.

Tiger Lily folded her long legs underneath her, kneeling on her bedroll and holding them in the morning light. She sat like that for a long time, and then, before walking out, she slipped the bracelets onto her wrist, like she knew she would be required to. It was as clear a message as any that their marriage was still on.

Outside her door, the children had made a pile of rocks. There were dusty fingerprints on her house where they had touched it and run away.

The women were preparing a boatful of fermented caapi

water for a ceremony. They did this by sitting and chewing and chewing crushed caapi vines. It was one of the things Tiger Lily hated most, because it required sitting still for so long.

She sat with them, and a few eyes drifted to her wrist.

Aunt Agda handed her a vine to chew, but with a warm, sorry glance.

Sometimes Tiger Lily's heart beat for her village. This was one of those times. They could believe her to be cursed, fear her and whisper about her. But they still cared enough to sympathize with her.

A faerie heart is different from a human heart. Human hearts are elastic. They have room for all sorts of passions, and they can break and heal and love again and again. Faerie hearts are evolutionarily less sophisticated. They are small and hard, like tiny grains of sand. Our hearts are too small to love more than one person in a lifetime. Aside from rare instances, like in the case of my father, we are built to mate for life. I went back to the burrow many nights, and watched Peter. I tried to talk sense into my hard little heart. But it had landed on Peter, a creature two hundred times my size and barely aware of me, and there was no prying it loose.

Without Aunt Fire to spy on her, Tiger Lily escaped as often as she could, but she didn't go back to the burrow. Maybe she feared there were different ways of being trapped than the ones she already knew. She often spent the mornings before the rain set in looking for snakes and then going to lie down in a meadow not far from the outskirts, where she could watch the clouds.

She was sleeping in the tall grass when we heard a papery noise—grass rubbing against itself—and she sat up rod straight.

I saw him before she did. He was emerging from the edge of the woods, with something brown and furry squirming in his arms. He wore a worried expression as he studied Tiger Lily. In his muddled thoughts I could catch that he was nervous to see her, though I didn't know why.

The squirming shape he held was a tiny, mewling wolf pup. "Her mother is dead," he said. "Caught in a trap. I thought of you." He walked toward her through the tall grass. Moths and grasshoppers burst into the air with every step. "The mermaids can't take him of course." He smiled, teasing.

It had been weeks since she'd seen him. His brownish hair was shaggier, but he was freshly washed. His skin was pale and he looked thoughtful, his forehead crimping, the breeze blowing at him and making him squint in the sun that filtered now and then through the clouds. He was wearing a pair of English pants that he had no doubt recovered from the shipwreck and cut off at the knees. I waited for him to look at me like he had before, but if he noticed I was there, he made no sign of it.

Tiger Lily suddenly caught his meaning. "*I* don't want him. He's an animal."

"So am I," Peter said, shrugging. "I've got fur." He pointed to his head. He grinned. "And feet. So are you."

Tiger Lily blinked at him. To the Sky Eaters, there couldn't be more difference between people and the animals.

Peter knelt next to her, and held the pup out by its armpits, so that it squiggled and licked its own nose. She looked at the tiny helpless creature, but didn't move to take him.

"Are you impressed I tracked you here?" he asked.

Tiger Lily sank back on her hands, unsure. Tracking came to her as easily as breathing. "Should I be?" she asked earnestly.

Peter dropped his chin, looked down at the wolf pup, and finally up at her again.

"Do you want him?"

"No." She shook her head.

"But he'll die."

"You take him."

Peter knelt, and his shoulders sank. "I can't. I'm not good with living things. Or taking care of things. Or being that nice. Or anything like that. The fact that Baby's still thriving is a miracle. I'm not much of a girl."

"People say I'm not much of a girl either," Tiger Lily said. She thought of Tik Tok, who was fond of saying that people were all bits of each thing, boy and girl.

Peter waited, then laid the pup in her lap. Then he moved its thin black lips as if it were talking. "Please love me," the wolf said, with Peter's voice. "If you don't, I will probably die a horrible death."

Tiger Lily didn't give him the looked-for laugh, but she let her hand fall onto the wolf's head. She felt the soft warmth of its still forming skull.

Without a word, she had agreed to take the wolf, and Peter saw this agreement, and smiled to himself. "Moon Eye will want him," Tiger Lily said. "She wants to mother everything."

"Moon Eye's the spindly one. Pretty. You didn't tell me you were the daughter of the shaman." Peter petted the pup and leaned in to hold his nose to its fur, smelling it and giving it one small, gentle kiss.

"How do you know?" she asked.

"I spied on the village." He ran a hand through his hair and pushed it lopsided, stretched out his long legs. "I've been spying for a while. Ask the wolf, he knows."

He went to move the wolf's lips again, but Tiger Lily cut him off. "People in my village think you're a monster," she said. She didn't add that they thought she was a monster too. She also felt both proud and irked that he thought her friend was pretty. "You have to stay away."

"I'd rather not."

Tiger Lily frowned at him. She didn't understand why she felt so suddenly protective of him. "I can make you." She was serious, but Peter grinned.

"With what?"

"With this," she said, and moved her hand to the hatchet at

her waist. But Peter only looked pleased.

He studied her face, and pondered for a few moments.

"So you're a brave girl?" he asked.

This startled her, made her nervous. She nodded, unsurely. "Yes."

Peter smiled now, triumphant. "Good. Then I want to show you something."

She didn't have to go. But she tucked the pup against her skin, in a fold of her tunic, and let Peter lead her.

I fluttered up into the trees to escape the eyes of a kite that had just come to circle above the meadow, and caught up with them a few minutes later, walking through forest I was vaguely familiar with, skirting a bog and a tangle of low, impenetrable bushes. From the sound of it, the river was nearby, but hidden in a crevice. They ducked under a massive, felled tree that I had passed in my hunts before. Its trunk protruded over a waterfall, its roots disappearing behind it.

Tiger Lily peered over the edge of the falls. The water poured out and pooled far below, deep indigo blue and white froth inside a ring of jagged rocks. "Can you dive?" he asked.

She nodded. "Yes." She and Pine Sap had practiced as children, day after day. But as a girl, she wasn't allowed.

"Can I see?" he asked quietly.

"Yes." Tiger Lily nodded.

She handed him the pup. She hesitated for a moment,

unsure of why he'd made the request. The drop was enormous. And then she stepped up onto the fallen tree, edging to where it hung over the abyss. She sucked in her breath, a few times, for she did feel a little bit of fear. And then she dove. She looked like a sparrow dipping for a mosquito, so graceful and smooth.

She hit the water with a splash, and her head emerged a minute later. Up above, Peter stepped to the cliff's edge to get a better view. And then he began climbing down to meet her as she climbed up the steep hill back toward the top.

When they met, they were next to a crevice that disappeared behind the waterfall.

Peter was quiet. Tiger Lily was soaked and catching her breath and she showed her white teeth to him in a rare smile. The water was dripping down her face and she pushed her hair back, coiling it behind her. With her cheeks flushed, she was almost girlishly beautiful.

Peter studied her for a moment, looking perplexed. "None of the boys will go in here," he finally said, gesturing to the crevice. "They're scared they'll get swept away." He scooted onto the ledge that led behind the curtain of water.

"It's a terrible offense to a waterfall god, to look upon its face," Tiger Lily said.

Peter grinned. "No gods behind here. Come on."

Tiger Lily had never heard anyone say this. To Sky Eaters, gods living behind all waterfalls was a matter of fact. But she clearly didn't want Peter to do something she wasn't brave enough to do.

He led her inside. She didn't know why, but she followed, tucking the wolf pup tight against her.

The water crashed just beyond their shoulders with immeasurable force. It was hard for someone my size not to help imagining what it would be like to be one drop in the deluge, flung from the cliffs above into an uncertain landing.

Peter smiled at her reassuringly. The air smelled thickly of dirt and earth and roots and wood and wet stone.

"I can't stay," Tiger Lily said, heart beating, moving to return the way she'd come. The place felt sacred.

"We can get out on the other side," Peter said. "This way . . ."

He walked her out where they had to duck. He tried to help her, but she climbed herself. It was darker here, and from the crevice above them I could hear Tiger Lily's breathing, and his. He was right behind her.

"Sorry. Are you scared?"

"No. I like it," she said, though she didn't say why. She liked that it was beneath the ground, where nothing seemed to change. She turned and smiled at him, and he smiled back, but more uncertainly.

They walked for a few minutes more, but increasingly there was something different, a charge in the air. The silence became heavy.

Peter moved to help her through the narrow upward

tunnel, help she didn't need, and the sound of the water became muffled now. The light was trickling down on her in two narrow slices, and as his hands moved to boost her he brought his face to her neck, almost as if he was bumping into her by accident, only he kissed the skin of her neck, just quickly. I don't think he'd been planning to do it, or that he'd even thought of it until that moment.

She went still as an underground lake, and waited for him to pull away. And when he did, looking surprised at himself and slightly embarrassed, Tiger Lily didn't meet his eyes but kept her face tight. She coolly hoisted herself out into the open air, and walked away on silent feet, clutching the pup to her chest. I fluttered behind her. I could hear that he didn't follow her.

Somehow, it seemed Giant would know. It was the tangibility of his maliciousness, which could lead you to believe he had ears in the forest. So when I saw the ruckus in the village, people running around and everything disheveled, Moon Eye wringing her hands at the gate and everyone watching for Tiger Lily, then tugging at her clothes to pull her in, I knew with a heavy heart that they all knew what had happened behind the waterfall, and that Giant could have her killed for betrayal.

So I didn't feel the confusion and shock of such a greeting until I saw the object of the chaos: it had walked into the village through the gates, held its hands above its head in surrender, and brought with it more danger than Peter ever could.

He was kneeling on a blanket near the fire. No one had dared go near him to try and put him back together, though he was clearly broken. He was emaciated, and it seemed that if the rags of his clothes came apart, he would, too.

Miraculously, his spectacles had arrived intact with him. When he spoke to Tiger Lily, she swayed on her feet.

Because before he spoke, she knew him. The Englander. Phillip. Alive.

SIXTEEN

In those early days that he was with the tribe, Phillip spoke to people we couldn't see. He tossed and turned as if his body was a burden. But it was no wonder. I had never seen something so mostly dead and still walking.

Tiger Lily was, of course, chosen to take care of him, though the villagers' curiosity was quickly winning out over their fear now that he was in their midst. They admired the foreigner's courage; following his tracks down to the ocean, Stone and some of the other warriors learned that he had been living in a cave, probably unable to climb to higher ground because of a broken leg and broken ribs, eating what shellfish he could find. Walking into the treacherous woods must have been an act of desperation, and he'd been lucky to find the tribe. But they would not go near him. They established him in a house on the edge of the settlement, far from the river's edge.

Tik Tok could not watch someone suffer and not try to heal him. So together, despite Tik Tok's fears of aging, he and Tiger Lily concocted potions and salves, soups and broths, and began to try to nurse the Englander to health. They stayed up nights so that if he needed someone, they were there.

Pine Sap insisted on visiting too. "If you catch something, I want to catch it too," he said one night to Tiger Lily, when they stood outside the dim hut, arguing. Moon Eye hovered at the doorway and watched with big eyes but was always too scared to enter, the wolf pup—whom she'd named Midnight—tucked into her apron. As Phillip's hut was the most interesting place to be in all the village, I took up residence in a clay cup near his bedside.

Beliefs in the village could be a funny thing. Curiosity inspired the villagers to wonder if they didn't want to believe in the aging disease after all. It was whispered in some circles that its contagion was just a superstition, and the earliest converts to this way of thinking were able to summon their courage enough to spy through the windows of Phillip's room. The village was so small, with people so tight-knit, that when an idea took hold, it took hold of everyone. Which did make it easy, sometimes, to convince them of something all at once.

Finally, three days after he'd come, Phillip woke from his

haze, focusing on the room around him. Tiger Lily knelt by him in relief. Moon Eye scurried away like a mouse.

I knew Tiger Lily was thinking about the kiss. She thought about it when she was washing her hair and when she was cleaning Giant's room, when she was breaking thread with her teeth for her clumsy weaving and when she was walking to the house and feeding Phillip soup.

For the next couple of weeks she held Peter like a secret in her heart, lying right under her necklace. I could see him written on her face, and Tik Tok, too, seemed to catch shadows of him, because he'd stop to stare at her, puzzled, as if he'd just seen the boy flit across her eyes—seen the ghost of the kiss lingering for a second on the skin of her neck before disappearing.

"What are you thinking of?" Tik Tok asked one of these times, when she was sitting with her back against the wall. He was embroidering her interminable wedding dress, though they were still in the thick of the rainy season, and the day of her wedding seemed an eternity away. He was wearing a regal woman's feather headdress and a dress of deep scarlet. That morning, he had felt sure enough of Phillip's recovery to turn some of his attention back to his hair, which he'd left loose and messy for days. Now he had braided it, plaiting the braids and wrapping them all around each other in waves so that the back of his head looked like a rolling, glossy sea.

The blush on her face was the color of the cave behind

the waterfall, the inside of the crevice, the backs of Peter's hands.

"Nothing."

Tik Tok stared serenely down at his work, the bone needle poking out from between his lips.

"Why is the Englander here?"

"We rescued him," she said, with a slow, questioning smile.

"No, why is he here, in Neverland?"

"I don't know."

"He never told you?" he asked.

Tiger Lily shook her head.

Tik Tok nodded thoughtfully. "Make sure he feels comforted. He has lost everything."

Tiger Lily turned her mind back to Phillip for a moment. "Before, in the stone house, he said that a ship would come looking for him."

Tik Tok took this in. "I hope for his sake that that's true and for our sake that it's not."

He laid his work on his lap and smiled softly. "You'll be a sight to behold in this."

She studied the dress, so feminine for her sleek frame, its lines of shells arching above each other like white waves. "Everyone will think I'm ugly."

Tik Tok smiled. "That's true. But we are a small village. We have narrow tastes. There's no telling who else in the world would think you're beautiful."

He rethreaded his needle, and they sat in comfortable silence for many minutes. Tiger Lily stared at Tik Tok's clock, mesmerized by its methodical ticking.

"Speaking of your wedding, Pine Sap is planning to poison Giant," he suddenly said, almost as an afterthought, like he was making a comment on the weather or what they were having for dinner. "You had better talk to him."

"I will." The punishment, of course, would be death. But it was clear neither of them truly feared Pine Sap would poison anybody. "He's a fool."

Tik Tok smiled again, indulgently this time. "Far less foolish than you. To not know what it's like to care for a friend enough to behave foolishly . . ."

But Tiger Lily was distracted, not concentrating on anything he was saying. It seemed like things were coming down fast. Her restlessness for life had disappeared, and now it seemed life was piling up on itself: Marriage. Phillip. The lost boys. Peter. She wanted to follow the kiss away from the village to the burrow. She wanted to escape in the ship that Phillip said would come for him. In either dream, one thing stayed constant. She smiled at the thought of Giant standing on the shore, wifeless.

She hovered on these thoughts all the time. I hovered around lives I couldn't have. And at night, I heard her whispering to the ceiling of her house.

"Forget him. Forget him."

SEVENTEEN

You may think my jealousy would have been enormous during those days after Peter gave Tiger Lily the smallest kiss on the neck. And you would be right. But these moments were swallowed by a bigger emotion, my tenderness for Tiger Lily, which had grown to take up most of the space in my body, without me knowing it. I can't say I didn't dream that this was a passing moment of infatuation, and that eventually Peter would notice and pick me—as impossible as that might have seemed considering my size. But I felt protective of Tiger Lily. I felt that just by watching over her, I could somehow keep her safe. And I wanted to keep Peter safe too. So I did the one thing I didn't want to do. I flew to the cove to watch the pirates.

From above, the world looks orderly. That is one of the

primary benefits of having wings. Being high shapes everything below into peaceful patterns. And even though you know there is chaos below, messiness everywhere, it is reassuring to sometimes think that it all eventually sorts itself out into something that looks elegant. My mother always told me I was too much like my father. That I had restless wings and that I was too nosy. But it wasn't curiosity that sent me to the cove, and I didn't think I'd like what I saw.

The pirates had chosen the cove partly because no one else had claimed it. It was located at the end of a partially bald tooth of land only slightly covered by scrubby trees, too swampy and mosquito-infested and ugly for any of the tribes to want it . . . though it did make a passable port. And it offered privacy. Here, the pirates could be as sloppy as they wanted. It had the smell of decay, discarded remnants of animals they'd eaten and worse. I surveyed it all with disgust, and held my breath until I got to the settlement itself, which was a smattering of roughly built log houses, and a central square for fires and meals.

I was surprised to see Hook with an emerald necklace on his head, the glittering piece of jewelry perched above his graying black hair. I recognized it from a pile of valuables in the stone house. I suspected that Hook wanted to see if any of the men would laugh, or ask him why he was wearing it. But the men just glanced at him sideways, nervously, and went about their work, which consisted mostly of drinking, sleeping, eating, and fighting.

"What do you think?" Hook asked, startling a man they called Spotty (because he was their default lookout) midstride. Spotty—thin, gap-toothed, and sunburned—looked visibly shaken.

"It's very handsome," Spotty finally said.

Hook pulled off the necklace, defeated. No one was ever honest with him. Smee appeared beside him with a plate of food in his hands, and suddenly he brightened. He motioned for Smee to sit.

"I don't see you enough, Smee," he said. "How *are* you?"

"Fine, sir." Smee was dabbing pork grease off his mouth with a napkin. It was a relief for Hook to be around someone with manners.

Hook patted him on the back. "You enjoying your drink?" he asked. Smee nodded.

"Well, frankly, I've lapped better off the floor of a bar," Smee said. "But I do appreciate it." Hook laughed.

I didn't like listening to Hook's mind. It tasted bitter and sounded scratchy. But I gathered a few pieces from his memory anyway. I learned that he used to care about a lot of things. He'd been well educated, self-taught. He used to have a passion for art. The world he had been born into had been a green one—farms, villages, and fields—and the one he had left in London had been gray, full of factories and grime.

Neverland had called to him out of legends. A green place.

A wild place. And most of all, a place where he'd never grow old. Most people in London hadn't believed it existed, but some still insisted it did, and Hook had cast his lot with them.

To get to the island, he'd begged, stolen, and eventually murdered. He'd searched for years. He'd become the things he'd hated as a younger man. So imagine his surprise when he'd arrived at long last, and realized . . . it didn't work. He was still growing older. The wilderness—so vibrant in his mind—was itchy and hot and deadly. And he, himself, had turned out to be more of a frayed, mediocre thief and a killer than an artist. Time had revealed to James Hook a different kind of James Hook from the one he had thought he was. And he had told all of this to Smee, over drinks, mostly failing to remember anything he'd said the next morning. And Smee had decided he was one of the most brokenhearted and miserable creatures he had ever known.

Down the hill, some of the men were getting drunk. Smee observed them dejectedly. A man named Alf was slurring endlessly about his father to anyone who would listen. Someone called Bill was trying to teach himself to read. Mullins and Noodler were bickering (Noodler, Smee remembered, still had a cut by his eye from the last time he and Mullins argued, with bottles). Cookson, addlebrained and in need of medical help, was looking for ants to eat, and Cecco was staring into a glass of cane liquor. Spotty was trying to play cards and having a difficult time because he was developing a cataract. And these were some of their strongest sailors. It was a pathetic group. Who else would have followed Hook all over the world's great oceans to live on a hot, hostile island? Smee wondered. Who else but him?

And yet, Smee had learned Hook had high expectations for people, and for himself: efficiency, courage, honesty. It seemed they never lived up.

It was Peter who'd been the last straw, when Hook had finally let his disappointment swallow him completely. Peter'd shown up, and stolen one of the boys Hook had taken on from London as a swab. And then he'd lingered over the years, stealing more boys, but also, and worse, reminding Hook of what he should have been. Because Peter appeared to be stuck at sixteen.

"It's the injustice I hate, more than anything," he'd said to Smee one night, his eyes red and glassy, slurring his words, his head lolling as he tried to focus. He'd vomited, and then promptly passed out on a bush. "I hate that the world does not work out fair."

Now, sober, Hook smiled at a man named Murphy as he passed, yelled, "You're the picture of health, Murphy! How do you do it?" then turned to Smee. "Murphy's an idiot, you know, classifiable. Anyway, I don't get to see you enough, Smee. Did I say that already?"

"It's nice to hear twice," Smee said.

"You've been out scouting. Any sign of the boys?"

"No." Smee shook his head. But there was something he

wasn't saying. And Hook could tell. The captain had passed his prime, but he was far from unintelligent. He could read faces. Even silences.

"You're holding something back, Smee? Tell me. I won't get angry." But the truth was, Hook could get very angry. Just last week, he'd killed the cook, suddenly and without warning. He'd been sorry afterward, but by then it was too late.

"I've seen the girl," Smee said. "She visits Peter, I am almost sure of it." I shuddered, making the patch of lichen I'd been resting against crackle, but of course no one heard. This, I hadn't known. I hadn't listened in the right direction to Smee's thoughts. But now I caught patches of the memory: Smee, hiding behind a ficus bush as Tiger Lily crossed into the forbidden territory. His fear at knowing if he followed her for more than a few steps, she would notice and most likely kill him. His frustration at having her so close and having no plan of how to obtain her.

"You're being careful, so she doesn't notice you?" Hook asked, then went on before waiting for an answer. "Sky Eaters don't ask for explanations. If she feels endangered, they show up and break the truce. We get beheaded. That's how it works."

Smee nodded. "I'm careful. I think she's keeping him secret."

Hook studied him for a long time, and Smee began to prickle all over, nervously. I could see a shadow of awareness pass over Hook, that Smee was keeping a secret too.

"You aren't interested in the girl still, are you, Smee?" Hook asked. Smee shook his head furiously.

"I'm not a fool," he asserted. I was the only one who knew for sure that he was lying. Hook sank back, and seemed to relax.

"I don't care if the boy is drowned, stabbed, or smothered . . . as long as he is gone." He ran his hands through his graying hair. "Keep watching her."

Smee dared to say it. "Of course, sir."

EIGHTEEN

Tiger Lily didn't forget Peter. And I didn't forget what I'd heard among the pirates. But how could I tell her? I reassured myself that her instincts were sharp, and that the likes of Smee would never be a match for her. Really, this was true. But it didn't stop a worry that threaded through me sometimes, that she or Peter would get themselves hurt. I hoped she'd spend more time with Pine Sap, around whom I always felt she was safe, even with his weaknesses. But the two barely crossed paths except at meals, when Tiger Lily was far away and Pine Sap clearly sensed his presence wasn't needed or cared for.

It took her two weeks to get back to the burrow. When she arrived, long after dark, a warm dot of light was bursting through the cracks in the ground, welcoming her. We descended down the passage, and found the boys in the den, playing a game of dice. Peter stood at the edge of the room with a saw, bent over a giant twisted root.

"He's building an addition," Slightly said.

Peter looked over his shoulder at her. He straightened up. "Welcome back," he said politely. He stepped forward and shook her hand, but he didn't look her in the eyes. And then, coolly, he turned back to what he was doing.

Only Nibs seemed to notice there was something off about the way Peter greeted her. The others gathered around Tiger Lily happily.

She had brought a sack of dried meat. Now she handed it to Curly. All the boys gathered around the sack, growling with excitement. Curly tried to get them to trade him compliments for the meat. "Tell me I am the supreme master," he said, dangling a piece between a thumb and forefinger, or, "Say you are sorry for anything obnoxious you ever did to me." But one look from Peter put an end to that. Still, it didn't stop Curly from tucking into his pockets a few pieces that he would later hide in little cracks in the walls of the burrow, to be retrieved at some unknown future moment.

Peter remained turned to his work.

"Everyone's going crazy tonight," Slightly said through a mouthful of meat. "The place is too small."

Nibs gave him a look. "We're fine," he said to Tiger Lily brightly. But Tiger Lily knew Slightly was right. Cramped together in one room, the boys all looked oversized, like giants.

After devouring the meat, they sat down to what they'd been doing, which wasn't much of anything. Tiger Lily sat next to Tootles on the dirt, and glanced sideways at Peter every few minutes, confused by his coldness.

"Can you bring some other girls sometime?" Tootles asked. One of the twins kicked his toe.

"Girls aren't like chickens, Tootles. She can't just *bring* girls."

Slightly began singing a wistful song under his breath, in a language I didn't recognize.

"French," one of the twins explained to Tiger Lily. "He's singing about a home in the hills. It's about a shepherd, sleeping the night with his sheep and thinking about his family in the village. At least, that's what he said it was about." The boys all listened quietly, though it was clear they'd heard the song many times before. And suddenly they seemed like very old souls.

One of the twins lobbed a handful of dirt at Tootles halfway through the song and, angry at the disruption, Slightly gouged up a handful and threw it back, but all the boys in the line of fire ducked, and the dirt landed smack across Tiger Lily's chest, splattering her neck, her chin, and her clothes.

"Enough!" Peter growled, turning from his work, though no one had thought he was paying attention.

He stood and took in Tiger Lily's dirt-spattered torso.

Then he turned a dark look on the boys. "Sometimes . . . ," he began, and didn't finish. Then he turned to Tiger Lily. His eyes on her made her nervous. "Let's go in the water. You need to clean up before you get home." With the boys trailing behind them, Peter and Tiger Lily emerged into the sounds of the darkness, all the trilling, rustling night noises. They walked down to the lagoon and then turned northward, following the shore to where the land widened into a sandy beach, marking where the lagoon ended and the ocean began.

Tiger Lily was too proud to show her confusion and hurt at Peter's coldness. "The mermaids will come," she said evenly.

"Not if I'm here," Peter said, as if it was obvious. Tiger Lily didn't want to let him be brave without her, so she followed him in. He was so bold as he waded deeper into the water, it was hard to imagine he didn't swim. But then, he must have had the certainty the mermaids would rescue him if ever he needed them. She had never seen someone so fearless. And she had always thought she was the fearless one.

The boys caught up and followed them in. All shirtless, they stood like statues in the low waves. They hollered to each other over the sounds of the waves, frolicked in the surf for a while, until finally and inevitably the tide moved them inland, into the mouth of the lagoon, where the water got warmer.

It was quieter now, and Tiger Lily and Peter fell behind. Up ahead in the darkness, the boys could be heard talking about their favorite pirate stories, afraid and pretending not to be. Their bodies were gangly in the shadows, mostly grown, but still growing.

They stayed close to shore, Tiger Lily swimming and Peter walking beside her, pulling himself forward with his hands like tortoise fins. The water droplets hung from his wet hair like diamonds. They passed the Never bird's nest, ingeniously built to float despite its heavy load of sticks and limbs and, eventually, enormous eggs. Some mermaids perched on a nearby shore, watching them with curiosity, but as Peter had promised, they stayed away.

As they moved through the water, the silence stretched between them. Tiger Lily didn't look at him directly, but I studied him from her shoulder.

Where on land Peter was a jackrabbit, in the water he was slow. Uncertainly, Tiger Lily slowed her pace to wait for him. She was thinking that she had never known anyone like him, and that he had kissed her neck and decided he hadn't liked it, or forgotten. She wanted to forget too. The water smelled muddy and thick, and they could still dimly hear the ocean crashing behind them. Tiger Lily rose and submerged, over and over, relishing the quiet of the darkness underwater. Only I could hear her heart beat fast in the dark. I floated on a lily pad whenever she went under, and rested on her shoulder when she surfaced again. Passing the time, Peter reached into the air and scooped me into his left palm, as if he were catching a firefly. I blushed.

Up ahead, Slightly talked as the boys swam close by.

And then, the crashing.

It all happened in seconds. A beast—enormous and covered in tough skin, like a rhino's—appeared through the undergrowth, just behind the beach where the two mermaids lay watching the swimmers. It snatched one of the mermaids into the air with its massive teeth as the other shot into the water to safety. The captured creature let out a loud, piercing screech. She flipped and struggled, but it wasn't enough. The beast charged back into the woods, carrying her in its mouth. Her screams continued for a few more moments, then went silent. Peter dropped me, and my wings hit the water.

And here is when something extraordinary occurred.

For a faerie, falling into water means you are as good as dead. I tried to lift myself up, but my wings were waterlogged and glued to the lagoon's surface. I could feel my legs dragging under.

Faeries have ways of telling each other things, but all of these involve the slapping together of our wings. I slapped mine feebly against the water, and I knew no one would hear me; to Tiger Lily and Peter it would just be a tiny noise, unimportant. But just as they were retreating, I saw Tiger Lily pause, and turn around, and swim back. I didn't even hope she was coming for me, so impossible was the idea to fathom. But suddenly I felt the water change underneath me, and her hands scooped me up as I caught my breath. She looked at me directly and without a change of expression, then quickly laid me against her shoulder, careful to spread my wings flatly against her. She waded up toward the muddy beach. Peter was still staring at the opposite shore.

The boys were all frozen, in shock over what had just happened.

"Did you see that?" Tootles asked ridiculously.

"It was horrible," Slightly said.

They all chattered about what they'd seen, amazed and thrilled at the power of nature. They didn't notice Peter was silent, or when he slipped out of the water and walked back to the burrow.

Tiger Lily watched him go, and then slid out to follow him. I tested my wings. The water had mostly slid off of them, but I stayed where I was, resting as she walked.

When Tiger Lily found him in the kitchen, Peter was sitting in a corner, holding Baby and singing to him just under his breath, so I couldn't hear the tune.

"Did you know her?" she asked. He shook his head.

He tousled Baby's hair, then looked up at Tiger Lily. "The woods have rules." He put Baby down gingerly in his trough with his bottle. "But the rules are ugly."

"It's nature," she said thoughtfully.

"I have a lot of disagreements with nature," he said, looking confused, and his downy brows wrinkled over his eyes.

She walked up to him and put a hand on his forehead, as

if he had a fever. It was an impulsive movement. She didn't understand him, or herself.

He moved his arm around her waist and pulled her close and placed his head on her stomach, as if there was something to listen to there. His concentrated, worried look softened.

She let her hand rest on top of his head.

He gazed up at her, every trace of the vicious hunter gone, his eyes wide and unsure.

"You didn't come back."

"No," she said. "I couldn't," she stammered. "A man arrived."

Peter looked at her. "I thought you weren't coming back," he finally said.

"I'm sorry," she replied reluctantly. I had never heard her apologize for anything. Even now, it came out in a murmur.

"We're together, right? You are with me. You'll come back again now, for sure, right?"

She nodded, her body softening in relief. She felt suddenly, violently thankful. He held himself against her tighter, and breathed into her suede tunic. She didn't think of Giant right then. When she thought of it later, she wondered how he hadn't come into her mind at all.

"I've never seen anything like you," Peter said.

I was too absorbed by my own thoughts to feel envious of Peter's arms around her waist, and the way he clung to her.

It's not that I was angry at him. He was a scattered, distracted boy, and I knew he hadn't meant to drop me.

Really, I was thinking about Tiger Lily pulling me out of the water.

You think you know that someone sees you one way, and barely at all, and then you realize that they see you in another. That was the night I realized Tiger Lily had seen— really seen—me all along.

NINETEEN

The oldest people in Neverland had banded together and lived in a remote corner of the island inhabited only by dinosaurs. They were called the ancients. They were those Neverlanders who had survived beasts, floods, river crossings, and the heat and diseases of the island so that now they were centuries old.

Peter asked Tiger Lily if she would like to go see them, and she said she would. He explained that Slightly had told him that he should take her to do something alone together, and that that was the first thing you were supposed to do if you wanted to be with someone. "It doesn't mean we're together forever or anything," he'd added, blushing. This particular outing would take three days, which Slightly said was exactly the right amount of time. There was envy in the eyes of the boys as Peter explained it all to Tiger Lily.

And so Tiger Lily told Giant she was going off on a woman's journey, and she simply asked Tik Tok if she could have three days to herself, no explanation. Because he trusted her, he consented. They set off one morning before dawn, with sacks of food attached to their belts.

Their path cut a big swath across the island, near the forests where the cannibals lived and below the pine-covered mountain homes of the Cliff Dwellers—as far as Tiger Lily had ever gone (on shaman trips with Tik Tok). Beyond that, the forest was so dead and dusty that people rarely traveled there.

As they walked, they each kept a secretive eye on the other. Tiger Lily watched Peter's hands as they traveled from leaf to leaf of the trees they passed. Peter's eyes, I saw, continually touched her two crow feathers as they swayed, the long thin line of her back pouring up to her neck, the graceful swiftness of her legs.

They kept apart from each other, but it was as if a string attached their fingers, because they could each feel each other's hands even though they carefully kept their hands apart. I knew because I could almost see that invisible string, could practically swing from it. And the more Tiger Lily's fingers tingled in his direction, the closer she kept them to her body, away from him. For miles, Peter asked if she wanted or needed to slow down. But Tiger Lily couldn't have been less tired. She was too awake.

As they walked, he told her stories, filling the empty spaces, and talked about the pirates. "I'm glad they exist," he said. "It gives us something to focus our energy on. And it makes us learn to be sly." The rationale didn't quite make sense to Tiger Lily, but she respected that it did to Peter. She told him about the truce the pirates had with her tribe, but he already knew.

Along the way, she picked plants for them to eat, pulling tamarinds from low branches, cracking open palm nuts to share. She showed Peter how to find hog plum, and how to chew on the stem to get the juice out. She grinned at Peter around the stem sticking out of her mouth, making a face, and he laughed. "We don't have people to teach us those things," Peter said. "Maybe if we did, we wouldn't be so hungry all the time."

"I'll teach you," Tiger Lily offered with a shrug of her shoulders.

"Did your mother teach you?" he asked.

"I don't have a mother," she said. "Like you." For some reason, Peter was glad to hear it.

That first night, they made camp in a cave. They wouldn't reach the ancients until the following afternoon.

After they ate, they sat on the dirt floor by their fire and listened to the noises outside. A wolf howled somewhere far off. Tiger Lily had cut her knee on a thornbush, and she rubbed at the wound unconsciously.

"Peter, why don't you think the pirates are dangerous?" she asked.

Peter looked at her. "I know how dangerous they are. But I don't want the boys to know. I think it's probably a matter of time really, till they find us." He looked up at her. "I want the boys to be happy. How could they be happy knowing?"

Tiger Lily took this in with worry. And Peter picked at tiny pebbles on the ground. He looked up at her from under his eyebrows.

"Something about you makes me feel like I can tell you things like that. You're so still. It's like, you'll just hear it." He smiled wryly. "I can't even hear what I'm thinking most of the time," he said, his brow wrinkling. "My brain's noisy." He was right about that.

"But you're so happy," Tiger Lily said.

"Yeah, I'm happy," Peter said brightly to the fire.

They sat and looked at each other.

Peter gave her a crooked smile. "The way I see it, ignoring things is important."

Tiger Lily thought about home, and her engagement. Peter's eyes turned to me.

"Why does this faerie follow you everywhere?" he asked. "Do you think she's plotting to murder you in your sleep?" he teased. My wings and the tips of my feet tingled with anger. But then he reached a finger toward me gently, and the anger melted. "Let's name her Tinker Bell," he said, like I was their child. He swooped his hand underneath me. "Hi, little Tink." Hearing him say it thrilled me—a name Peter had invented, just for me.

Tiger Lily nodded. "Okay." Peter let me go, and turned back to her.

"I've never had someone like you around before. What do people do who are together?"

Peter could be like that, so suddenly guileless that it caught at your heart. Tiger Lily held her breath and said nothing. I could see that her approval meant the world to Peter, and that he was hanging there, waiting for it.

"Peter, I shouldn't keep coming to see you. I'm supposed to . . ."

Peter shook his head hard, annoyed. "If you have reasons for not coming back, I don't want to know them. I just want you to come back anyway. Ignorance, see?"

Tiger Lily sat still as Peter crawled toward her and settled beside her, looking at her cut knee. The way he stared for so long at her knee made her blush, and she knew he must see it. He put his hand on the scrape, which hurt and made her flinch, and then leaned forward and kissed it, then sat up and kissed her lips, hesitant at first and then with more force.

Peter sat beside her and kissed her for a long time. Tiger Lily's heart was racing, her thoughts a blur. Then he abruptly pulled away. He seemed upset with himself for being so little of a gentleman, and moved to the other side of the cave to sleep. I knew Tiger Lily would rather have held on to him, to keep him next to her a little longer, but she let him go in silence. I watched him pulling off his shirt to go to sleep. His chest was concave. There was a long scar on his lower back. And a little birthmark on his stomach.

Tiger Lily had already turned to the wall, and they both pretended the other wasn't there for the rest of the night. I lay in the crook of Peter's arm for a while, and could see he didn't sleep but only closed his eyes. I watched his eyelids flutter, the creases and the fine rims. And then I went and settled into Tiger Lily's hair and drifted off. In the morning she woke to Peter crouched beside her, studying her, looking tired.

"Time to get up," he said.

They reached their destination at midday.

Everything here was old and overgrown. The ferns were enormous, big enough for a person to use as a bed. The insects were thick and swollen. The dragonflies were five times my size, and I hid in Tiger Lily's hair, though if she felt me trembling, she didn't act like she noticed.

Tiger Lily didn't feel these were her woods, and neither did I. They slowed their pace, and seemed to anticipate something jumping out at them at any second. They climbed a rise, which promised to crest just beyond the tree line.

Almost at the same moment they reached the top, a horn blew. They hid themselves in some tall grass, and looked down into the small valley.

Below, there were the ancients, or a group of them, gathering. Some had a shock of white in their otherwise dark hair. Others looked very young. With my sharp eyes, I could see that many had grown their finger- and toenails impossibly long, now brown and crackly and old looking. They moved slowly toward each other, one foot in front of the other. They stood still together, and one minute passed into the next. They stood and stood.

"I don't understand why they move so slowly," Peter said, troubled.

"Maybe when you're so old, you don't have any places to hurry away to," Tiger Lily said. She felt guilty. It seemed like they were looking on a private sight not meant for their eyes.

They lay watching for a long time, and the ancients barely moved. Occasionally one would wander into the group, or wander away, but generally they stayed together and did very little.

"So that's what it's like to live forever," Peter said. For reasons I didn't know, there were tiny tremors in his muddled heart.

"Well," he said.

"Well."

"Let's go," Peter said. And, unceremoniously, as if they hadn't walked for miles and miles to see the sight, he turned and began walking away. Tiger Lily watched him for a moment, surprised, and then caught up with him.

*   *   *

That night they slept in the open, by a fire Peter had lit. Peter didn't kiss Tiger Lily except on the forehead, and he retreated to his bed quickly.

The next day he was quiet for the whole walk home. But at the place where she was going to say good-bye, and when he seemed to be thinking of something else as she turned to go, he suddenly pulled her close and hugged her tight, and rested his chin against her cheek. "Thanks for coming with me."

Tiger Lily made her attempt at a smile. After having felt the need to glower at other children for most of her life, smiles never came easily to her face. But this one was half all right.

"I miss you already," he said.

Tiger Lily wanted to say it back. But she held on to the words greedily, too caught in the habit of keeping herself a secret. And Peter—half sadly, half expectantly—let her go.

TWENTY

T he rains began to let up a little more each day, and one morning Tiger Lily came out of her house to see the sun winking at her as she walked into the middle of the village. The hot season had arrived. This was usually Tiger Lily's favorite time, when the jungle—having soaked up the rains—was at the height of its greenness. It lasted for about the cycle of three moons. But today, it worried her. She knew at the end of it lay the dry season, and her marriage.

Phillip had taken to walking the village, or rather, hobbling it. People kept a wide berth when he came shuffling down a path they shared, and pressed themselves against the houses on either side to let him pass. But they had also adopted him as a sort of pet.

"What's the white one up to this morning?" Silk Whiskers,

one of the older warriors, would ask as he watched him walk by the well or sit by the fire, and the others would pipe in with their latest observations.

"I saw him yesterday whistling at a parrot," Stone would say.

"He has walked that circle eleven times by my count," Red Leaf's brother, Bear Claw, would throw in.

Still, weak and slow as he was, the village was starting to catch the shape of Phillip's personality where it overflowed his wispy edges. He recoiled from too much raucous laughter. He wrinkled his forehead when the men drank caapi water, and looked concerned and unhappy as they were transported into deeper and deeper trances. He was clearly put off by Tik Tok's womanly dresses and hairstyles. During the day, Tiger Lily still brought him food and sat with him. Occasionally Tik Tok showed up with a potion he'd mixed for a speedy recovery, and each time, Phillip stared at him like he was a foreign creature, and a puzzling one. He kept a very spare bed. He didn't eat meals with the tribe but just ate the grain and beans plain. While everyone gathered at the riverbanks to fish, he would bring the one book he'd arrived with and read, which made the villagers poke each other and laugh quietly as they watched him. He was kind, and smiled gently at the children. He didn't seem to grieve for his lost ship and his lost life with the same wild, inconsolable terror and pain that the villagers seemed to feel at loss.

But the most striking thing about him was his control

over and denial of his body. The villagers painted their bodies with messages and meanings—they liked to tattoo themselves with symbols, painted their faces to mean different things. Phillip seemed to float above his body, like it was just an attachment. He didn't seem to revel in the food Tiger Lily and Tik Tok faithfully brought him, or fresh air, or dangling his feet in the river on hot days the way the villagers did. The only things he took pleasure from seemed to hide somewhere in his head.

He spoke to Tiger Lily from time to time, singling her out.

"I've never experienced a heat like this," he'd murmur, fanning himself and his sweaty, shiny bald head. He told her about his wife back home, who had died three years before. "She settled for me," he admitted one afternoon. "I always knew she loved someone else. But God works in mysterious ways." Tiger Lily listened to all of this patiently, only half understanding the things he meant. She wanted to ask questions, but there were too many to begin. She was proud that he was alive partly because of her. And tending to him was a welcome respite from her other duties in the village.

Since his mother's death, Giant had gone from tolerating Tiger Lily to actively hating her. He purposely made messes for her and created extra work that sometimes kept her up late into the night so that she couldn't go to the burrow at all. He liked to berate her in front of others, and in private—because Sky Eaters had no tolerance for men hitting women—he had even tried to knock her down twice with a slap. Though much to his frustration, it was almost impossible to knock her over.

Tiger Lily was invulnerable. She wrapped her secret around her like a blanket, and it kept her warm over the next few weeks, when people in the village eyed her, or whispered in their usual way. Tik Tok often looked at her, puzzled, while they sat to eat or mix medicine together. But he didn't ask her any questions. It was his way to wait for her to tell him.

She was carrying boiled water to Giant's house one afternoon when she noticed Pine Sap slipping out of the village with a hatchet.

"Where are you going?" she asked, just at the tree line.

"For a walk." His spindly arms clutched the hatchet, his feet rooted firmly and his stance listing slightly to the left because of the subtle curve in his spine.

"With a hatchet? Into the woods?"

"Yes," he said, daring her with the smile that grew on his face. "Don't worry, Tiger Lily, I'm not going to look for poison for Giant."

"You'd be a murderer," Tiger Lily said.

He leaned on a hip. "Tik Tok always exaggerates. I don't have the heart for murder. Let me help you with that."

He took the bucket of hot water from her before she could resist, and they dropped it off in Giant's empty house. "Let's go somewhere before he gets back."

So deep was her distraction that she didn't wonder again about the ax he'd been taking into the woods.

They walked down to the bend in the river. It was a brutally hot day—even the breeze was hot—and the cool river water, trickling down from the mountains, was too inviting to ignore.

Without a word, they both started undressing.

Tiger Lily went in before him, impatient. But Pine Sap knew her impatience well, and didn't expect her to wait for him. He followed her upriver. They blew on the grass blades to make them whistle. She gave him a wet smile, and her smile made her beautiful. Her teeth were as white as shells.

She sank underwater and held on to Pine Sap's calf.

They waded into a batch of reeds. The river had carved natural paths through the tall river grasses, so that there were miniature hidden trails they loved to travel, knowing no one in the world could see or find them. For others, this might have felt lonely, but for Tiger Lily and Pine Sap, it had always been a welcome respite from people's eyes.

"Where do you go to at night?" Pine Sap asked suddenly, softly, as if the answer didn't really matter.

Tiger Lily sank her mouth under the water, then raised up slightly. "Red jasmine, for stomach problems. You have to gather it at night." She said it so quietly that anyone would have known she was lying. Especially Pine Sap, who spotted lies so well.

"It's okay," Pine Sap said. "You don't have to say." They were quiet for a while. "Do you like Phillip?" he asked.

Tiger Lily nodded.

Pine Sap shrugged. "I don't."

"Do you think you'll catch aging?" she asked.

He shook his head. The villagers believed less and less that aging was something they could catch. "It's not that," Pine Sap said.

Tiger Lily didn't pursue the thought further. "Maybe he will take me with him to England, when the ship comes to take him back," she said. She hadn't dared voice this thought to anyone.

"You'd leave the tribe?" he said.

"Instead of marrying Giant? Yes," she said decisively. The idea that going away on a ship would mean saying good-bye to Peter didn't enter her mind.

"I could never leave," Pine Sap said.

"Why?" she asked.

Pine Sap shrugged, and gestured in the direction of the village. "Because I think people must be the same everywhere. Only these people are my bones."

Tiger Lily hovered, her mouth open as if to speak. But I don't know what she would have said, and at that moment Moon Eye walked by, Midnight in her arms—though he was already growing way too big to be carried. She looked like her thin bones would crack under his weight. It was an infectiously charming sight, and Pine Sap smiled big at her.

"He's not a baby," he said.

"He is sort of my baby." Moon Eye stared down at the wolf in her thoughtful way, with a little motherly smile.

"Come in the water," Pine Sap said. Moon Eye smiled gently but shook her head.

But Tiger Lily climbed up—covering her torso with one hand and dripping all over—and put wet hands on Moon Eye's cheeks, and together they got her to put the wolf down and coaxed her into the river, in her tunic. Midnight sat on the shore and whined, spoiled already.

Moon Eye came into the reeds with them, and they all spit water at each other. For a moment, Tiger Lily felt jealous, because the reeds had belonged to her and Pine Sap, and because Pine Sap smiled so much at Moon Eye, who had so many of the traits Tiger Lily never would, like softness, and breakableness. But for a moment, she also felt so at home in the village that she let the jealousy slip out of her fingertips, and she even almost forgot about the burrow and Peter entirely. But only almost.

TWENTY-ONE

I f I'd never really known Tiger Lily was an animal, I knew it now. Tiger Lily was a beast, and the boys were too, and they were beasts together.

She resisted, at first, giving in to all the things the lost boys gave in to. The way they lay on the leaves for hours while the villagers would have been hard at work cultivating their crops, making improvements on their homes, and squirreling away food for the rainy season. The way they covered themselves in mud when they got hot, while the Sky Eaters liked to clean and groom themselves three or four times a day. How they pushed each other out of the way when they wanted to get somewhere and how they sometimes grunted instead of spoke. But it all worked on her, and slowly she let herself get dirty and unruly too.

It was easiest to slip away right after dinner, when villagers were busy catching up with each other and broken into their separate, small groups. So, though from time to time she was able to get away for an afternoon, evening was burrow time. She could stay away till long after the Sky Eaters were asleep, and those who noticed she was gone, like Pine Sap, or Tik Tok, would assume she was avoiding Giant.

I fell into the habit of looking after the boys. What else could I do? Curly had long since lost interest in smushing me, so I got bored of simply flicking my earwax into his food or hiding briars near the groin of his leggings. I started to clean up after them as much as I could. I moved the little knickknacks they left lying around to places where they'd be easiest to find and use. I joined in when they chased each other, though no one ever noticed when I caught them, landing on their shoulders. Still, it was intoxicating to imagine being a part of their lives, even if they didn't think of me that way.

I watched Tiger Lily eat with the boys, sloppy and greedy, until they all had stomachaches. It wasn't unheard of for Tootles to eat until he vomited. She covered herself in leaves like they did to take after-dinner naps, emerging with a muddy, dirty smell that she always had to wash off at the seaside before she went home. One evening I heard a foreign sound, like a boar choking, and discovered it was the sound of Tiger Lily's laugh. From then on, Tootles made her laugh often, breathlessly, something I had never seen in all my years of watching her. Nibs, inquisitive but never pushy, could make her soften and almost open up about herself. She told him about Tik Tok, and together they wondered about what had ever happened to her parents. With the boys, she liked to sit with her legs splayed boy-style as they did while they ate or lounged, and no one seemed to notice or care. I suspected she was an inch away from running around with her shirt off too.

Simply put, she ran wild. Or that's what the tribe would have called it. She wrestled with the boys like a monkey. She didn't always win, but she could hold her own. There were many things she could do better than them: she had better aim than everyone but Peter, she could run faster, but they didn't seem to mind. And she didn't seem to mind when the boys touched her—hugged her or tackled her or punched her in the arm—though for years I'd seen her let few people so much as pat her shoulder. She didn't mind when they ruffled her braids or poked at her two crow feathers, even when Curly liked to steal one and stick it up his nostril. "You seem to be missing your feather," he'd lisp to her through the feather hanging out of his nose and down over his lips, as if it weren't there.

It wasn't that they didn't treat her like a girl. I knew from my previous visits to them that they always tried to be better when she was around, always let her eat first. But they tormented her too, like they constantly tormented each other. And as far as I could tell, she loved it.

Every night, she crossed the bridge over the crocs, and it began to feel familiar and safe. Her nose was more sensitive. Her senses felt sharper than ever. I kept an eye out for watching eyes, and saw nothing. I told myself that if Smee were watching, one of us would have known it. But the forest was deep and thick, and sometimes I wondered if even Tiger Lily was sharp enough to notice everything.

When she could get away during daylight, they brought her on hunts. The lost boys went about hunting a whole different way than the Sky Eaters did. They stopped often: to lie in a meadow, to pick berries, to fling dead stuff at each other or wade in creeks. They meandered. They argued and fought. Especially Slightly and Nibs, or Slightly and anyone.

Sometimes Peter treated her like she was the only thing in the forest. Sometimes he was so distracted by the things around him that she had to keep up or be left behind. But a lot of times, she knew he did it on purpose, and she didn't know why. He seemed to have reasons for doing things even he didn't understand.

How can I describe Peter's face, the pieces of him that stick to my heart? Peter sometimes looked aloof and distant; sometimes his face was open and soft as a bruise. Sometimes he looked completely at Tiger Lily, as if she were the point on which all the universe revolved, as if she were the biggest mystery of life, or as if she were a flame and he couldn't not look even though he was scared. And sometimes it would all disappear into carelessness, confidence, amusement, as if he didn't need anyone or anything on this earth to feel happy and alive.

Peter in the creek was dazzling. He could hold his hand so still in the water that fish would swim right into it; he almost seemed to talk them into his hands. He showed her how to do it, as he would have with any of the other boys; he simply seemed to take it as his duty to teach her. He could climb anything—even, it seemed, sheer rock: he'd find the invisible places where his toes would fit. He knew how to emulate the call of the howler monkeys perfectly. Where the boys all watched for snakes and scorpions under their feet, Peter didn't slow a bit, nor did Tiger Lily when she was stubbornly keeping pace with him. He never seemed to think over a decision, but merely plowed ahead, and somehow the earth always caught him in her soft hands. No one thought of doubting him.

But, most dazzling of all, he was weak around Tiger Lily. I realized this one afternoon when he was watching her eat red berries they had picked at a favorite patch of bushes beyond the edge of the territory. The red berry stains on her lips seemed to practically torture him with their beauty. When he sat beside her, aching to be close to her, she smushed some berries onto his face, almost shyly. He tackled her around the waist and she rested her chin on his shoulder tentatively, and he nervously touched her face and traced it. It was like this sometimes, and I felt I should look away, but I couldn't. I wanted to be there, having my face touched, defeating a heart like Peter's, but the next best thing was seeing it for Tiger Lily. Peter would grow helpless. He watched her with Baby when she thought no one was looking—she'd poke the baby curiously, and stare at him with fascination and a little fear. Peter spied on her at the village taking care of Tik Tok. He liked to watch her run. And always, I could see that, despite his weakness for her or because of it, he seemed uncatchable, as if he might slip away at any moment.

An unspoken rivalry threaded their relationship, in which Tiger Lily thought that if she could keep up with him, she could hold tighter to him. It didn't occur to her there was anything in which Peter wanted her to fail. But sometimes I could see that, even for him, she was too fast, too sure-footed, and didn't seem to need him quite enough.

And sometimes, when it was quiet and the boys had wandered off somewhere, he'd pull her close, as if he was about to say something, and they'd kiss each other. I would always look away, longing and sad and caught up in their happiness all at once.

Peter was working on a wooden flute for Tootles one night in the burrow. He was increasingly frustrated with the wood in his hands. It was obvious he wanted to finish it, but he hated sitting still. And the work looked painstaking.

"He won't finish it," Slightly whispered to her. "He never finishes anything." He shook his head, long-suffering and annoyed. "Trust me. *Anything*."

I was carrying different tools to Peter, hoping they might help. Every once in a while he'd look up and say, "Thanks, Tink," focusing on me for a joyful moment. I treasured these seconds when Peter acknowledged me, and I tried to seek out other things he might need or want, in order to get more of his momentary glances.

"Did you notice life has gotten better?" Tootles asked, out loud, to anyone.

"It's Tiger Lily," Slightly said, as if Tootles was being an idiot. They didn't say anything about me, but I decided to believe they meant both of us. "Life's better with girls. Boys need girls. That's why things are so boring in the burrow."

"You should move in with us," Nibs said to Tiger Lily.

Tootles snaked his hand behind her elbow and leaned against her, innocently and thoughtlessly, but when Peter's eyes darted to his fingers, Tootles let go, then just patted her on the shoulder.

"I want to see buildings sometimes," Curly said, out of the blue.

"I dream of living in a house. And girls," Slightly said, then added solemnly, "and also . . . did I mention girls?"

"Shut up." Peter stood suddenly; let out a loud, angry sigh; and stalked off. As predicted, he left the unfinished flute behind.

Then he came back, shoulders stooping. "I'm sorry," he said, to the ground. Then walked out again.

"It must be you," Nibs whispered to Tiger Lily, who sat erect against the burrow wall, uncomfortable. "He never comes back and apologizes."

Tootles picked up the pieces of his abandoned flute.

One morning at home, Tik Tok had Tiger Lily try on her wedding dress. He seemed disappointed that it fit so well. Despite their expectations, it became her. Its simplicity and sleekness were subtle enough to highlight her strong, high cheeks, the shine of her hair. It was a dress made by someone who knew her. It was her freedom and her silence sewn into a dress.

She hated what it meant. But she loved the dress because it was from Tik Tok's hands and because it made her feel like herself. She took it off.

At night, Tiger Lily tossed and turned, feeling like Peter was beside her all the time.

TWENTY-TWO

Phillip surrounded the villagers with stories, and whether they were make-believe or not, the people of the village wanted them to be true, because they were hungry for someone to tell them the way things were outside. He enraptured them with talk of England, and mapping the world, but mostly what they wanted to hear about was heaven, and they argued late into the night with each other about what it looked like and what and who was there. They began saying their prayers. I could hear them at it, their thoughts lifting up above the rooftops, promising God they loved him best, which Phillip said was important, though they muttered, in whispers so that God wouldn't hear, that it seemed God must be unsure of himself to need so much reassurance. Still, Phillip said God could see them all the time, so they were careful.

Almost no villager, in those days, liked to start their day without going to listen to Phillip tell his stories after breakfast. The women came and embroidered and shucked corn as he talked, and the men stood respectfully and absorbed his words before going off to hunt. Pine Sap was one of the exceptions. He came to listen once, early on, and then chose to go into the woods instead whenever Phillip was giving his talks.

"You see, your island is so isolated, things have come to live here that don't live anywhere else," he explained. He told them about the animals in England. But mostly he talked about things of the spirit.

He said God meant things. So when a baby was lost in childbirth, he said God had meant it. To the villagers, this seemed to indicate that God had meant for Aunt Fire to die too. So everyone began to fear God was a vindictive spirit, but Phillip said that wasn't correct, that he was protecting everyone.

"It's all part of a plan," he said, and smiled. "Our reward isn't here on earth. Earth barely matters. It's just practice. This life is only a passing place, a stopping point, on our journey."

Tiger Lily thought about Peter and his wild ways and wondered if he ever suspected he was just inhabiting a passing place, and whether those ways would keep him from going to heaven. Though even with all the danger that seemed to surround him, it was impossible to think Peter could ever die. She shivered at the idea.

There were a few things that Phillip said God didn't like. He didn't like naked women running around in public. He didn't like people thinking about other gods. And he didn't like people loving objects. So the Sky Eaters packed up their beloved carvings and engraved rocks and trundled them off to bury them so they could come back and find them later should their entry to heaven be assured. God didn't like that Tik Tok wore women's clothes, either, though Phillip hadn't said this. Still, everyone began to guess.

Phillip scratched his bald head and smiled often at these gatherings. His baldness glinted in the sun. Tiger Lily wondered that God didn't whisper to him about her visits to Peter, because he seemed to talk to God often, and to know exactly what God thought and wanted, whereas the villagers never knew what the gods wanted at all, though they had listened and listened and still found that the gods' wills were always a mystery.

Like Pine Sap, Tik Tok did not stay for these talks. He escaped to the nearby meadows to gather roots. One afternoon, Tiger Lily went to help him. She had missed the last two times he'd gone. Every time she looked up, he was watching her, and then he quickly looked down at his work again.

"Tik Tok, why don't you listen to the stories?" she asked.

Tik Tok leaned back on his haunches, and thought for a moment. "Everyone wants to be sure, but I never am. I'd rather sit here and not know things. It's bad of me, I know."

He gave her a conspiratorial wink. Tik Tok had limitless patience, but he was a poor listener when he didn't like what he was listening to.

They stopped to eat two strips of deer meat he had brought in his sack. He'd misplaced the bigger sack in which he'd packed a fuller meal.

"You look happy," he said suddenly, and met her gaze. She quickly looked down at the roots again, sorting them into her leather waist pouches. "But tired."

Her late nights with the boys, and her duties during the day, were taking their toll. She walked through the village oblivious and even clumsy. She'd dropped a wooden bowl on Red Leaf's head the previous morning. She had nicked Giant while cutting his hair, and infuriated him to the point where he struck her in the face. Moon Eye had stood watching like a statue, and then insisted on taking the knife up instead, because she said she had more sure hands, even though they'd trembled the whole time.

"For someone who is marrying someone she hates, you look very alive."

She silently chewed her food. Tik Tok studied her—but his gaze was so open that it didn't make her uncomfortable.

"Pine Sap is a nice boy, and he loves you, but remember, you are engaged to someone else."

Tiger Lily looked up, shocked. "Pine Sap?" She watched the expectation on Tik Tok's face. "I wouldn't think of it. And he wouldn't think of me."

Tik Tok stared at her a long time, then shook his head, as if to himself. He allowed himself to be befuddled for a few moments, and then he gathered himself and spoke.

"Whatever you're doing, whatever is making you so happy, I'm glad about it. But if it's something that can't fit with your marriage, if you're not honoring yourself and us, you'll have to give it up. What are we if we aren't people who keep our promises? We're nothing. We're like bugs," he said, pointing to an ant on a piece of bark, scurrying along mindlessly.

Tiger Lily looked down at her dirty hands. Her fingers trembled, just slightly, but enough for a loving, observant man like Tik Tok to see.

"Oh, my little beast, I'm sorry." He suddenly looked uncertain. "I trust you. I want you to be happy. Maybe I don't know what I'm saying. Maybe I'm not so wise."

I'll tell you a terrible secret. I was down at the water washing my wings that evening when I saw two figures, just as the sun was going down. Moon Eye, going down to bathe when she thought she would be unwatched, and Giant, a moment later. She struggled, but this time she didn't get away.

After he was gone, she dipped herself in the river—a shivering, frail, skinny creature—resolved to hide better, to stay farther away. But over the next weeks, there was nowhere he wouldn't find her.

She never told.

TWENTY-THREE

Sometimes Peter and Tiger Lily fought. A fight between them looked like this: Peter, head swirling with anger, waving his arms around and expressing five thoughts at once about why she was wrong and he was right; Tiger Lily, curling up inside like a rock, stone-faced, listening but at the same time refusing to hear. She hated his need to always win and he hated her coldness during their arguments. They fought about the exact color of the sky and which path they should take on a hunt. They disagreed passionately about whose fish was the best tasting. They could work up extreme hatred for each other at a moment's notice. "I'm nothing to you, am I?" Peter said once in a particularly intense argument about where to find wild turnips. To these kinds of accusations, Tiger Lily would reply that he was trying to make her into his little chicken, and that she would never be anyone's "little obedient chicken"—as if there were such a thing as an obedient chicken. The lost boys were befuddled by these fights, but came to roll their eyes and sigh and make themselves disappear at the appropriate time. I, too, learned to ignore them, even when one of them stalked off in the opposite direction of the other one and headed for home. When they made up, it was as if nothing had happened at all. In fact, it was like they were stuck even closer together, like they had gotten even more tangled in each other.

One night, after making up, they found themselves across the lagoon, on a thin slip of ground between a bubbling hot spring and the lagoon's flat water, lying on their bellies, staring at their reflections in the water. Throwing rocks onto lily pads.

Steam rose up and coated their faces with moisture. Phosphorescents floated under the water. I sat on a dead leaf and relaxed, keeping an ear to the night noises.

The heat of the water made Tiger Lily feel like the night air was cool. A breeze gave them goose bumps. They could see the stars above, between the branches of some thin trees. Here, Tiger Lily felt for the moment safe, like nothing could ever touch her or them. But Peter spoke of the pirates.

"They've been coming too close to the burrow," he explained. "Just one set of footprints. We've never seen them get so close before. They've tracked us as far as the edge of the glade. They can't know where we are. But we want to know what they're up to. Don't worry. I'm not scared of them."

It comforted me that he had noticed, at least, that someone had been nearby. But he didn't seem concerned. He was more preoccupied with Tiger Lily.

Peter liked to look over every part of her: her wrists, the strands of her hair, her ears, the tiny creases in her lips. And she was no better. She memorized the tiny constellation of freckles to the left of his nose, and the scars on his knuckles, the fan of his eyelashes, the many expressions of his face. I knew them almost as well as she did, because watching him love Tiger Lily was better than not watching him at all.

She stared into the still surface of the lagoon. Nowhere near her village was the water so glassy, and she could see her face in the surface—her broad cheekbones, her strong nose, the black line of her hair. Beside her, Peter was fairer.

Peter twirled his finger into the water image of his face, making it break apart and reassemble itself over and over again. He had promised the mermaids would leave them alone on this side of the lagoon, though she expected a jealous, slimy hand to rise out of the dark wet and grab her by the neck at any moment. Still, if Peter was going to brave such proximity, so was she.

"What's the Englander like?" he asked finally.

"He is old. He has no hair on his head." She smiled.

Peter sighed into the water, and his breath sent a small circle of it into tiny ripples. "It seems cowardly, getting old. Don't you think?"

She rolled onto her side to look at him, pillowing her ear with her right arm, and letting her fingers dangle in the water beyond her head. "How is it cowardly?"

Peter kept his eyes on his reflection. "You just curl up around yourself, and sit by the fire, and try to be comfortable. When you get old, you just get smaller inside, and you try not to pay attention to anything but your blankets and your food and your bed."

"Being comfortable is not a bad thing."

Peter shrugged and turned his head to look at her as if it was a matter of fact. "Of course it is. Old people lock out all the scary, wild things. It's like they don't exist."

She wanted to say that she would have liked for those things not to exist, either, but she held her tongue, because she didn't want to sound like a coward. She had been thinking of Giant, and the pirates. Sometimes she wished she could lock them out and just be secure.

"It's like now, we could be in our beds, safe. Or we could be here, staring into the black water of the lagoon, listening to the sounds of the insects, with the twigs pricking our stomachs and the danger of death by mermaid at any moment."

Tiger Lily shook her head. "But the English can't help it if time passes and they get old."

Peter wrinkled his nose. He yawned. "There's no such thing as time passing. That's an excuse."

"No it's not." She sat up, smiling at him. "It's true."

"You can't prove that."

She thought. There was no way, she supposed, if you didn't believe getting older was part of time getting older too. And then she remembered. "Yes." She nodded. "Tik Tok's clock. It's a machine that tracks time with its hands."

Peter looked suddenly curious. "What's it like?" he asked. Everything Peter asked, his body asked too. At this moment it slumped, in defeat, at such a beautiful idea, and also leaned forward eagerly.

"The clock has little hands that point to the minutes, very steadily. It keeps a perfect record of time."

She could see he was trying to grasp that the moments in life and everything in it could be held in a little wooden box.

"Can I see it?" he said, his face lighting up.

"I could never get it from Tik Tok. He wouldn't let it out of his sight. It's his most prized possession, besides his hair." She smirked at him.

Peter sank. "I'd give anything to see time."

She grew silent, because what could she do?

"You're so quiet when you don't know what to say. Always."

"You don't even know me always," she said. But he was right.

She slid next to him.

Peter put his hand on her rib cage. And just looked at her. He swallowed. "I love you so much, Tiger Lily," Peter said. Tiger Lily stiffened, stared at the ground, and said nothing. A smile spread across her face, but she didn't show him.

They just sat in silence for a long time, until finally Peter stood, looking uncomfortable. "I'll walk you to the bridge." She was startled to see, about ten paces on, a lump in the water that, as the moon passed from behind a cloud, showed itself to be Maeryn, watching them. The mermaid sank silently and quickly underwater.

"Meet me at the bridge tomorrow night?" Peter said. "I don't want you to come to the burrow, until we figure out what's happening with the pirates."

"Yes."

"Are you cold?" he asked. She nodded. He pulled off his fur vest and gave it to her.

He rubbed her arms with his hands, stood his warm feet on her cold ones for a few moments so he could take the cold and she could take the warmth. "It's okay. I'm always warm." Then he shivered as he walked.

Up above, I listened to them. I could hear their hearts. Tiger Lily's, I knew well: her unsure, stumbling happiness, her fear of knowing about something so beautiful as Peter. But imagine my confusion at listening to his—Peter, so perfect and courageous—and hearing a fear in him that seemed to dwarf hers.

If there was a true moment that Tiger Lily fell so in love with Peter she could never turn back, it was that night, when he shivered and walked and told her he was warm, and told her he loved her so much. She was fierce, to be sure, but she had a girl's heart, after all. As she walked home that night, she was shaking from the largeness of it. I didn't know why she seemed so sad and happy at the same time. To love someone was not what she had expected. It was like falling from somewhere high up and breaking in half, and only one person having the secret to the puzzle of putting her back together.

She began to plan how she would give him up.

TWENTY-FOUR

S he waited for Peter at the bridge the next night, turning over what she would say, and I played tag with the fireflies. But Peter didn't come. Since he had asked her not to go to the burrow without him, she walked just to the edge of the lagoon to see if she could spot him.

Tiger Lily noticed Maeryn after I did. She stepped closer to a tree, defensively. The mermaid was sitting in the mud just at the shoreline, staring at her. She had a skull cradled in her arms. "Pirate," Maeryn said, smiling, as Tiger Lily lowered her hand near her hatchet.

"I don't want to kill you. I'm curious about you." She was the very picture of feminine mystery. All sharp teeth and soft lips.

"Watch that boy," she said. "You're stronger in many ways,

but that doesn't mean he can't take you apart."

The first thought that went through Tiger Lily's mind was that she was not stronger than Peter. "He wouldn't do that," she said.

"He won't mean to. He just won't be able to help it. It'll be an accident. It's in his nature, just like it's in my nature to live underwater." Tiger Lily knew she couldn't trust Maeryn. Wasn't she the mermaid who supposedly loved Peter most of all? And now Peter loved Tiger Lily. Still, she couldn't help being fascinated.

Maeryn eyed her, then seemed to ascertain something surprising. "You're keeping a secret."

Tiger Lily stepped back, halfheartedly shook her head.

Maeryn waved a hand above the water carelessly. "Oh, I don't care. It doesn't concern me. Only Peter does."

She glanced in the direction of the burrow. "Peter loves to make promises. He has the best intentions of keeping them. It makes it worse, somehow, that he doesn't know how to. He thinks he's a nice boy, that's the worst part."

Tiger Lily didn't understand. Instinct told her to go back the way she'd come, and she did. But before she was out of earshot, Maeryn said, in a low, perfectly confident voice, "I'll be here if you need me. And you will."

Almost everyone was down at the river the next afternoon, catching salmon. The island had slipped into the thick of the hot season, a time when the salmon swam upstream and it was easy to catch them. You could dip your basket into the water and it would come up filled with fish, which the villagers would then spend the next several days smoking and drying.

Down on the banks, everyone who wasn't fishing was gathered around Phillip. The village seemed to have forgotten their fear of him completely. He was talking about how only fish should be eaten on Fridays, and how Tiger Lily's marriage should happen indoors, in a chapel they would build. People laughed at first, because they thought he was joking. How would God see them if they were indoors?

Tiger Lily came across Moon Eye sitting on a rock off the path to the water, with her needle and thread, Midnight ensconced beside her and hanging on her every movement with his yellow wolfy eyes.

"Why aren't you down at the river?" Tiger Lily asked.

Moon Eye usually liked to do her work by the water, on a fallen tree where she could watch the fish and listen to the hawks eat their midday meals. She shrugged. "Why aren't you?" she asked.

Tiger Lily looked down at where Giant sat by the river, part of the group and apart from it. She didn't need to say why.

Moon Eye made a spot beside herself for Tiger Lily. Tiger Lily sat and studied her beautiful work: a long suede skirt, adorned with a bird flying skyward.

"It's your wedding present," Moon Eye said. The bird looked like it was escaping, transcending earth. But

Tiger Lily's attention was drawn to Moon Eye: she looked disheveled, as if she hadn't bathed for a few days. She was usually as meticulously clean as Tik Tok.

Moon Eye looked down at the group by the water. "You should talk to them. It seems they want to believe anything that man says. I don't trust him."

"You sound just like Pine Sap," Tiger Lily said. Their eyes traveled to Pine Sap, who was in the river up to his waist, fishing. His chest was so skinny and frail compared to all the other boys'.

"And why would I be the one to convince them not to?" Tiger Lily asked.

"People are nervous about you, but they respect you."

Tiger Lily shook her head. "No."

"And you're Tik Tok's daughter. They respect that. Though . . . ," she added, "they turn to Phillip for advice now."

Tik Tok was not near the river; Tiger Lily didn't know where he was. But she had a feeling he wanted to be somewhere away from Phillip's lessons.

"I wish I were brave like you," Moon Eye said suddenly.

"Why do you say that?"

Moon Eye shrugged. If Tiger Lily hadn't been distracted, she might have noticed the seriousness in her tone. As it was, she just shrugged it off. Moon Eye was often incomprehensible to her. It was no wonder Pine Sap had grown such a fondness for her; they were so much alike.

And Tiger Lily felt a moment of comparison in which her bullish ways came up short against Moon Eye's thoughtful, gentle ones. At the moment, she didn't feel very brave. She was trying to think of a way she could possibly bear giving up Peter.

In the water, catching their fish, the villagers looked so happy. Aunt Sticky Feet put her arm around Red Leaf and gave her a squeeze. Pine Sap was kneeling in the current, helping some of the children position their baskets under the water. He rarely came back from these fishing forays with a catch because he spent most of the time like this, helping the little ones. With them, he seemed at his most confident and lively, and the children of the village—who were always so scared to come close to Tiger Lily—flocked to him like bees to a flower.

Tiger Lily thought about what Tik Tok had said, about promises, and who she was if she didn't live up to her duties. She didn't notice Pine Sap jogging up the hill until he was standing in front of them, dripping, a large salmon dangling from his right hand.

"For my mother," he said, holding it up. "I'll smoke it, so it keeps for a while." He ignored the look that crossed Tiger Lily's face. She was disappointed in his weakness, his eagerness to appease his mother, and it embarrassed him. "Hey," he went on, falsely bright, "will you help me practice spearing tomorrow morning, before everyone's up? I have to go on the hunt, day after. It'd be nice if I made it through the day without being a laughingstock." He smiled abashedly, his brows knit together.

Tiger Lily nodded. "Yes, I promise," she said.

"Great. I owe you." Pine Sap beamed. He winked at Moon Eye, then hurried off with his fish, his wet feet slapping on the path. Moon Eye watched him go, but Tiger Lily didn't. She stared down at the bird on the skirt. She wondered if there was any way she could fly away too.

TWENTY-FIVE

I woke in the night to a figure by Tiger Lily's bed. It was Peter kneeling beside her in the dark, watching her. She woke with a prickling feeling.

"I'm so sorry I didn't meet you at the bridge, Tiger Lily. I'm sorry."

"You shouldn't be here," she said, fear running like lightning down her legs.

"Come with me."

Tiger Lily wanted to say no. But she got up and followed him. The village was sound asleep, and the only light was a faint orange glow from the dying coals of the main fire. They didn't make a sound, though I could hear Peter's breathing, and they didn't speak until they'd crossed the threshold of the forest into the trees. And then, he only said, "The boys are waiting up ahead."

The boys stood in a gaggle by a creek a safe distance from the village, and huddled around a tiny fire they'd built. In the firelight I realized Peter had painted his face. They all had.

"Why are we—"

"It's an adventure." Peter gave her a big, hardened smile and started walking. It chilled her. They all followed behind him.

After a few minutes, Nibs fell in step with Tiger Lily. "We're going to the pirates," he whispered, giving her a meaningful look and swallowing nervously. "They've gotten too close. We saw more tracks, just on the edge of the territory, but we lost him. We're sending a warning." Startled, Tiger Lily looked to Peter for confirmation. He didn't meet her eyes. He wore an unrecognizable expression: his pupils were huge, and his face was cold, like a mask of himself. The others looked scared, and Tootles seemed like he was going to be sick. One twin kept glancing at his pale, green-hued face. The other twin, Nibs explained, had stayed home to take care of Baby.

Tiger Lily didn't tell Peter that she couldn't go, that she'd never get home before morning and that a Sky Eater breaking the truce and provoking the pirates was dangerous for her whole tribe. If he was going somewhere dangerous, she wanted to be there with him. He smiled his strange, cold smile at her, from far away. She'd never seen him look so frightening.

They slowly entered the part of the island that was lower lying than the rest, and more empty and rocky. The boys' fear became tangible as we saw the first landmarks of the cove—a few torches stuck in the ground, unlit, with skulls on top. I hate to say that just below them, like a kind of trim, were several hundred faerie skulls. I wondered if they belonged to anyone I knew or had known, and shuddered. The sight of the skulls slowed the boys' feet, too, and Tootles began to shake. Peter pushed forward at the same pace, seeming to forget we were behind him. Tiger Lily hurried to stay beside him. Unconsciously, she kept a hand on her hatchet.

As we came to the outskirts of the cove, Peter finally slowed, became stealthier and even more silent, and grinned at the boys, looking more in his element than maybe I had ever seen him. I could tell we'd come within range because it smelled like rotting meat, and within a few minutes we arrived at the place where the pirates threw their animal carcasses. They'd clearly been lazy about their butchering, and left some valuable parts of the animals to rot, as if the killing—of something as "lowly" as an animal—made no difference. Tiger Lily found this shameful, and her heart hardened a little more as she walked.

We came to a long narrow walk between tangled mangrove trees. Peter walked ahead. Tiger Lily followed just behind him, keeping her eyes trained on the thick foliage. I could hear Peter's familiar breath.

And then he came to a stop. Tiger Lily saw a split second after he did.

The man was curled up on the ground, his dirty white shirt just visible through the trees. He lay behind an intricate construction of bamboo and spiked spears, cocked and ready to release at whoever was walking down the path.

A bottle was curled into his elbow. He was asleep.

It was all so quick that Tiger Lily didn't have time to stop it.

Peter pulled back a branch, whether to see better or to move closer, it was hard to say. The man woke. It took him a second to make sense of what was before him, but the moment was too long. Before he was upright, Peter had a thin rope around his neck. The man jerked, reached for his neck, struggled, kicked, and made a gurgling, tortured noise. It lasted for what seemed like forever, though it could have only been seconds. And then, almost just as quickly as waking, he quieted, and his life ebbed out of him.

When Peter stood to face the others, he was panting and triumphant and shaking with fear. Tiger Lily stood staring at him, in shock.

They walked toward home in silence, and the Peter who had killed a man began to fade, so that the Peter we knew emerged. He became quieter, slower, more thoughtful in his movements, noticing the dark, angry presence beside him.

"You're unhappy with me," he said flatly.

Tiger Lily lifted her chin. Her anger was so palpable, even the boys took a few steps away from her. Her heart was as cold as ice.

"He was ready to kill us." Peter smiled hopefully, but it

bounced off the steel of her face and dropped.

They didn't speak for the rest of the walk. The other boys were uncomfortable with their discord and walked on ahead in silence. Nibs kept glancing back at them. Slightly and Curly argued in a hushed whisper over who was going to eat a coconut Curly had pulled from his sack, their appetites undeterred by recent events.

Tiger Lily walked with Peter to the burrow but, once there, changed her mind about being there, and walked into the darkness. Peter let her go, but then came after her a few moments later, startling her as she reached the top of a small rise.

"Please, Tiger Lily." He pushed his hand into hers and she let the fingers stay loose. "You think I'm a monster."

"No." She shook her head, keeping her own thoughts.

"But you believe in killing. If your tribe was attacked."

She turned her eyes on him. They were so full of disappointment that Peter flinched. "There are rules to killing," she said. The Sky Eaters, when they went to war with someone, sent a series of warnings. To sneak, to ambush, was so foreign to someone like Tiger Lily, she couldn't fathom it.

Peter looked desperate. He held tighter to her hand. "Tiger Lily, the pirates take young boys. They're usually orphans. They snatch them up and put them to work on their ships. They're slaves. They beat them and worse. Slightly was nine when he was taken. He still remembers. . . ."

Peter's voice trailed off, and he swallowed. She listened in silence.

"When I met him, he'd escaped. I saw him in the woods, and he was so skinny and lost. But I took care of him. We rescued the others, over the years. And now . . . I have to scare the pirates. To protect the burrow."

I felt Tiger Lily thaw, but only slightly.

"Peter, how did you get here?" she asked.

Peter looked down at his hands. "I don't remember. I have a bad memory. You know how people remember a few things that happened to them when they were small? Slightly does, even Nibs and the others do. I don't remember those things at all. I just remember being here."

"But to sneak up on someone and attack them is cowardly."

"To not do what you can to protect someone, that's cowardly. You wouldn't understand. You don't have to be afraid of anything." He kicked a root protruding from the ground, then sighed and gave her a softening look. "I need you to think I'm okay," he said.

Tiger Lily was silent beside him. She took hold of his hand. She wasn't sure what love was, but maybe she was supposed to bend. "I think you're okay," she whispered. From the burrow behind them, they heard a burp echo out and reverberate in the trees. They couldn't help but smile.

"I think that's the biggest compliment you've ever given me," Peter said ruefully. It gave Tiger Lily a twinge of guilt. She regretted that she wasn't better at telling people how much she cared about them. But Peter looked as if a weight had been lifted off his shoulders.

Tiger Lily sighed. She was wrapped in Peter now, and she didn't know how to extract him from herself.

Peter went back to the burrow to see to the boys, and she departed alone. The sun was just coming up. And there, like last time, was Maeryn, just her eyes above the water, staring at her.

She lifted her mouth above the water. "You're being watched," she said.

I realize now that she must have meant Smee. But that wasn't who Tiger Lily thought of. She remembered suddenly that she had broken a promise.

"You've lost your feathers," Maeryn said behind her. But rushing away, Tiger Lily didn't hear it.

TWENTY-SIX

T iger Lily hurried along the river, looking for Pine Sap. She didn't often walk this far upstream, as it became tangled and impassable. But now she heard a hammering, camouflaged by the sound of the water. Following the sound, she came up to a small structure, crafted even more carefully than Tik Tok's house.

Pine Sap was on his knees, twining a piece of sinew around two poles. His attention was so wrapped in his work that he didn't hear her approach until she was almost above him. He startled. Then smiled up at her in his crooked, slow way and stood, brushing the dirt from his knees.

"What do you think?" he asked. He gestured to all of the poles and pieces of wood, the carefully scraped bark, the scrollwork, four walls.

"This is what you've been doing in the woods?" she asked.

He nodded, clearly excited for her to see. "It took a while, I'm slow at these things." But he was being modest. The work was astoundingly intricate. It was a proper house—with four walls intact, curved inward, and sitting on stilts. "I was going to wait a little longer to show you."

It was almost finished, except for the roof. It overlooked a quiet bend in the river, where the water slowed and collected in a small, calm pool, deep enough to swim in.

"It's beautiful, Pine Sap."

"You like it?"

She thought of the hours it must have taken him—while she'd been running wild, playing games with the boys, making the journey to the cove—and tried to understand how all that time, Pine Sap had been here in this same patch of forest, working on the same thing, day after day. "You have so much patience," she finally said, her voice falling tellingly.

"You say that as if it were a bad thing."

"No," she said, but the lie was detectable. "It's just . . . don't you get restless?"

Pine Sap looked nervous, and swallowed deeply. "Yes, but . . . it's worth it. To have something to show in the end."

"Yes." Tiger Lily nodded as if unconvinced.

He seemed to sense her disapproval, because he turned back to his work, his smile having sunk away.

Tiger Lily looked around. Up on the roof, a pair of crows

were perched, curiously watching Pine Sap work.

"Are those your friends?" she asked.

He smiled softly, then let out a tiny, eerily perfect caw and reached into his pocket, laying a handful of dark-purple berries on the ground beside him. "They love these," he said. The crows were there in a heartbeat, there by his side, gobbling down the berries. They had no fear of Pine Sap at all. But when Tiger Lily moved to kneel beside them, they flew off to a nearby branch.

She stood and laid a hand on one of the walls, tracing the designs of it with her fingers. "Why have you kept this a secret?"

Pine Sap sat back on his knees. "I don't want people to give me their opinions on it. It's where I want to live, when I'm married. I want it to be close to home, but far enough away from the gossip and everyone's eyes. Just a place to be ourselves."

She crouched beside him. "It's beautiful, Pine Sap. Really." She put her hand on his shoulder. She thought of Moon Eye in the house. How peaceful she would think it was.

He looked up at her a long while. "You think I wasted my time?"

"No, no. It's just, you and I are so different." She was thinking how bored she would have been, working on the same monotonous task.

"I hear you," Pine Sap said. He had heard more than she wanted him to hear.

She changed the subject abruptly, to what she had come to say. "I'm sorry I didn't come this morning."

Pine Sap nodded. "You're still going off at night," he said.

"I can't sleep. I go for walks." She let him infer the rest. She didn't lie all the way.

"Be careful," he said. He didn't believe her. But he didn't believe she would lie to him about anything important. "You could always run into something you can't handle. A jaguar or the lost boys or something."

Tiger Lily looked at her hands; the depth of her guilt seemed bottomless. "I will."

I talked myself into flying back toward the cove a few days later. I wanted to see the pirates' reaction to their lookout's death, and see if there was anything they planned to do about it.

I was surprised though, just beyond the forbidden territory, near the berry patch the boys often liked to visit, to run into Smee—far from the grotto and barely recognizable. He was tattered, swaying on his feet, tromping along loudly. I followed him until he sank down onto a rock, and I listened to his thoughts.

He had barely escaped the cove with his life. Hook had been drunk since the morning they'd found Spotty strangled on the forest floor. Of course, they all knew who'd done it. And Hook had proceeded to get drunk immediately, murmuring that at any minute Pan would materialize from the trees to murder him. He hadn't even picked up a weapon; he'd just gone into a bleak depression.

Finally, two days into his binge, he'd become convinced Smee was betraying him in some way. "I don't know what you're lying about," he'd said, "but I know you're lying." He had been too drunk to kill Smee. He hadn't been able to find his knife. So he'd cast him out instead.

Now Smee, huddled on the boulder below me, was alone. His frantic thoughts flitted from his inability to hunt to the fact that there was no one who would possibly take him in. He had come here because it was where he'd last seen Tiger Lily. It was the only thing he could think to do.

He was still lost in this thought when I heard loud footsteps crookedly winding their way among the berry bushes a few yards away. Smee ducked into the greenery. I lifted up into the air a few feet to see Tootles, trawling for berries. For every berry he dropped into his leather pouch to bring home, he shoved two into his mouth, staining his lips red. He was humming Slightly's French song.

He wasn't looking around him like the other boys would have. I flew over to land on his shoulder, to try to warn him. He recognized me, but flicked me away, shoving more berries between his lips. I tugged on his earlobe. He swatted at me.

Finally, he swiveled back in the direction of home. He walked, and Smee followed. My heart began to race. When Tootles didn't turn around, I flew to him, yanked on his hair, but he kept brushing me off and nearly pulverized me against a tree. And behind him I heard Smee's thoughts: that the boys were the way back into Hook's good graces, and his way to Tiger Lily, and that this was all too good to be true. When we reached the burrow, poor, dumb, hapless Tootles pulled up the tree stump so he could enter underground, without even a glance in any other direction. He happily climbed down into the hole, still humming.

I turned to look, but Smee was gone.

TWENTY-SEVEN

M irabella showed up one morning to convince me to come home. I was drinking water from a rose petal when she appeared at the edge of my nook above Tiger Lily's bed.

Back home, she had the worst nook in the worst log, where we'd once lived together. The holes in the bark looked out on a swampy piece of land full of mosquitoes. Together, before I'd left for good, we'd conspired to make our home more homey, hunting out sparkly rocks and flower dyes. But then I'd left and failed to come back.

Faeries can't speak to each other, but of course we read each other's thoughts. Mirabella was thinking that I'd been gone long enough. And I was thinking I needed to stay, to look after Tiger Lily and Peter, especially now. To Mirabella,

I knew, it seemed pathetic. She was convinced they didn't deserve me; they didn't notice me enough for me to even be able to help them, or warn them, she reasoned.

But my mind was made up. Mirabella lingered for a few minutes, waiting for me to regain my sanity. She sat on a twig and glowered at me. But finally, she flew off, annoyed. I flew off to find Tiger Lily, who was down by the river.

Aunt Sticky Feet was trying on shawls. Phillip had found them on the beach, washed up from the shipwreck, and she had dried them—moldy and threadbare though they were— by the fire.

"Do I look like an English lady?" she asked. Tiger Lily, sitting beside Moon Eye and Phillip on a rock, nodded. Beside her, Moon Eye was quiet, and picked at the threads between her hands.

"Are most people dressed English in heaven?" Aunt Sticky Feet asked.

Phillip laughed. "Well, it doesn't matter," he said. "It's what's in your heart that matters."

"What about if, in your heart, you wish bad on someone else?" Moon Eye asked, surprising everyone. She barely ever talked to Phillip. "Does that mean you can't go to heaven?"

They all looked at Moon Eye for a moment. She looked around at them, then said, by way of explaining, "If someone is a bad person?"

"It's not for you to judge someone else," Phillip said. "Judging isn't what God created us to do." Moon Eye took this in.

"But you judge Tik Tok for wearing dresses," Tiger Lily said. "You don't think God created him to dress like a woman."

Phillip looked sad. "We all have roles, Tiger Lily. You are a woman and you have a role. I as a man have a role. We all have to be the best we can be at the roles we have. We can't decide to switch. I feel sad for Tik Tok's confusion, but I know he will find his way."

Tiger Lily considered this. It didn't fully make sense to her. "But Tik Tok believes everything's circular, including men and women. He says nature seems to go around and around, and that we all have bits of everything."

Phillip smiled. "There *is* a beginning and an end," he said with certainty.

Tiger Lily tried to picture God in heaven, making laws and having things end with him. It didn't seem circular at all.

Later that afternoon, she walked into Tik Tok's house and sat on the floor. He was sitting with his eyes closed, smoking his pipe. He had done his hair in an ingenious crisscross pattern down his back, but messier than usual.

He was puffing on his pipe. Tiger Lily smiled. "Phillip says smoking is a sin."

He seemed to ruminate on this. "I don't believe it. I don't even believe in that good and evil. Oh—"

He had burned his finger holding the edge of his pipe. He looked at her sheepishly. "That felt evil." He settled back down, blew smoke from his pipe. "Maybe it's easier," he said, "to believe what someone else says is absolutely right."

"He thinks you shouldn't wear women's clothes."

This was no surprise to Tik Tok. He had known it for quite some time. He was quiet for a few moments, then turned to Tiger Lily. "Maybe you should talk to him."

"Me?" Tik Tok had never asked her for anything. It took her by surprise.

"He won't listen to me. Of course," he said with a weary smile, "we may both be too much like women for him to listen to either one. The only God is a man, apparently." He smiled wryly, but sadly.

Seeing Tiger Lily's concern, he patted her hand. "Don't worry," he said, laying down his pipe and arranging things. "I trust this village. Everyone will figure it out for themselves. But"—he looked at her and for a moment, the veil of his confidence lifted and revealed a foreign uncertainty underneath—"maybe you could say something for me. Just in case." It was such an uncharacteristic request that Tiger Lily didn't know what to say.

"Tik Tok . . ." She looked around the room, feeling nervous. "Do you ever think Phillip is right? Do you think maybe it's better if you don't wear dresses?"

Tik Tok looked at her for a long time.

"I just mean, maybe it would be easier? Then you don't have to worry about God." She immediately felt like she had said the wrong thing. But Tik Tok only nodded. His smile returned, but it wasn't real.

"You go out and enjoy the day," he finally said. "Don't worry about an old man like me."

Tiger Lily bent and kissed the top of his head and reluctantly moved to leave. As she walked out, she felt unsettled. She reasoned with herself. Tik Tok should do what made life easiest for him, and what would make things easiest was for him to change just one thing. But as she walked down the dirt path to her own house, she couldn't shake the feeling that she had let him down, and she didn't know how to change it.

TWENTY-EIGHT

Tiger Lily was especially restless when she escaped to the burrow a few mornings later, when she was supposed to be out harvesting manioc at a nearby field. Peter beamed when he saw her.

I whispered into Peter's ear that the pirates could be coming after him, right this moment, but of course my whisper made no sound. I tugged on Tiger Lily's hair. But I was only a nuisance to them. Smee hadn't resurfaced, and I didn't see signs of him anywhere near the burrow. There was a distinct possibility he'd starved before he could get to the cove, been eaten by some forest creature, or been killed by one of the other pirates. Still, I watched the woods, constantly, for signs of the pirates.

"We've been wanting to show you something," Peter said to Tiger Lily.

The lost boys raced through the woods, Peter and Tiger Lily in the lead. I kept up as best I could, thankful that I had wings, as Peter and Tiger Lily were tireless, and even the other boys began to drop behind, panting and clutching their sides.

They came to the bottom of a rise. Peter raced Tiger Lily to the top, each of them intent on beating the other one, their heels digging into the soft, crumbly clay as they climbed. Tiger Lily reached the top—a flat, wide, grassy plateau—a moment ahead of Peter, but he tackled her, pushing into her so that she fell onto his shoulder, and he carried her a few feet, dropping her and standing back to show her the view.

The plateau was a giant meadow, covered in tall grass and wide, smooth stones. The boys all collapsed, flattening the grass around them until they had a beautiful 360-degree view of the island below them. We could see to the shore in two directions, patches of green forest and the brown expanse of the swamp, even—very small and dark—the lagoon.

"It's beautiful," Tiger Lily said. Neverland lay before them as if it were theirs, and she could see the thinnest trail of smoke spiraling up from her village, and the sparkling line of the river. From above, it looked like you could walk across it all with a few giant steps.

The boys had packed food, and they pulled out every bit they had and ate ravenously. Then they played a game Slightly remembered, where you hid a piece of cloth, and guarded it with your life from the opposite team. Curly played a pair of wooden spoons he produced from his pocket, and all the boys took turns dancing with Tiger Lily across the smooth surface of stone.

By the time their bellies were verging on full, the sun was setting. Tiger Lily had seen many sunsets. The Sky Eaters knew every sunset by heart, because they'd watched each one, every night of their lives. They kept lists of them in their minds, and could even remind each other of a certain day by saying, "It was the day the sky was purple all the way up to the one cloud, the one shaped like a bird." Or, "That was the day the sunset was pink only behind Bear Mountain." But this was the most beautiful one Tiger Lily could remember. The sky went red and orange and pink and purple. The puffy clouds, shot through with the last rays of the sun, grew an inviting depth, so that they looked like they could be the caverns of Phillip's heaven. She imagined souls roaming the tunnels of the clouds.

"Look," Peter said.

To the north was a series of vast grassy plains, and there, just looking like specks at first, was a herd of horses, a species that in Neverland had never been tamed. They were beautiful, flashes of brown and black and tan, their coats gleaming. There was no reason for them to be running that Tiger Lily could see. It was likely that they just loved to run.

"That's what I want my life to be," Peter said, staring down at the horses.

Tiger Lily sank against him and watched the herd, and thought that was what she wanted too.

I am only a faerie. I don't have grand ideas, or grand dreams, or long for grand freedoms like people do. But I wanted to be part of their dream too, even if I was only a flea riding on their tails. To run and run and never worry—that was what they wanted, and I wanted to go with them.

I could hear the quiet in Tiger Lily's heart. I had never heard it so soft, so at peace, as I did that evening, as she sat with Peter and watched those horses, and dreamed for a moment that she would never have to lose him, or herself.

No sooner had the sun dipped below the water than a dim crescent moon began to rise. The boys were silent—everyone lost in thought, watching it make its slow climb upward. Peter put his arm around Tiger Lily and gently pulled her back onto the grass so that her head was in the crook of his arm and she was staring at the bluish-purple sky as it deepened, and the stars began to prick their way through the night.

She felt the warmth of Peter's arm under her neck, and it almost felt like he was an extension of her, and like if they had souls, they lay somewhere snug between their two bodies. Maybe all of her strangeness, her curse, her always feeling like an outsider, had all existed so that she could belong here, with Peter.

They watched until the stars filled the sky, as if there were more stars than darkness, and then someone finally moved, and they stood and stretched without a word, and made the long, listening walk home in the dark.

When we got back to the burrow, Peter announced he was going to bed.

"Can you stay?" he asked.

She stood there, bewildered.

"Where am I supposed to sleep?" she asked.

"Well, there are plenty of blankets everywhere."

The boys stood staring at them with open mouths. Tiger Lily looked at the pile of blankets on the floor, considered leaving. Then she felt Peter take her hand. Behind them the boys whispered, and Tootles giggled at something until Nibs shushed him with a pinch on the arm.

She let him lead her down the hall to his room.

He lay down on the bed and she lay down beside him, on her stomach. At first, Peter seemed unsettled. He wasn't used to sharing his space. He tried to stretch out diagonally, almost kicking her off the bed by accident, and then he seemed to collect himself into a tighter package, pulling his arms into his sides. "Sorry," he said, "it's a small bed."

She stared at all the little knickknacks he'd scattered about. Unlike the first time she'd seen his room, when everything seemed messy, she noticed now they were all carefully placed: the half-carved mermaid was watching over him from her spot in the corner, and I settled down next to her. The tiny wooden birds he'd never finished all faced the direction of the door, as if they were about to escape, or to protect Peter from whoever might walk in.

"You need to eat more, Tootles, you look like a ghost," they heard Slightly say from the hallway.

"Eat this," Tootles said, followed by a thud and the sounds of struggling.

Peter poked his head out the door. "Hey, you guys, shut up!" The hallway went silent, then the whispering of the boys retreated.

He came back. "They're like children," he said. "I'm not a great model."

He turned on his side and tentatively put his arms around her, as stiff as lobster claws. "I'm glad you're here," he said. She turned to face him. She let him lean his forehead against hers. She thought about going.

"I've had girls sleep over before. Macryn came and we put her in a big tub. But I don't know about you. What do I do?"

"I don't know."

He kissed her cheek.

Soon they could hear some of the boys snoring down the hall, and the stirring of the restless as they fought sleep for a last few minutes. And then it was quiet.

She turned her back to him, and Peter held her, hooking his chin over her shoulder, warmth coming from his chest.

"You'll be my wife," he said. He was trying to sound sure,

but there was a fear on the last syllable, and she felt his heart beat harder. "Forever."

She squeezed her eyes shut. She held his arms tighter around her. When Peter said *wife*, it didn't sound like being a prisoner at all. She thought about Giant. Would they wonder where she was? What if she didn't wake early enough to sneak home?

He waited for her to say something back, but she held her breath. Peter looked up at the ceiling for a long time, waiting, but in vain. His shoulders sank slightly against her, and he didn't let her go.

Finally she felt his breath go slow and steady, and knew he was asleep.

She learned that night what I already knew: that in his sleep Peter was a different person. He tossed and turned and worried out loud, making small groaning noises and, every once in a while, a cry. Sometime deep in the night, after keeping her awake with his fitfulness, he woke with a start, and in the near pitch-black he pulled her in tight, like they were in the ocean and she was keeping him afloat.

She felt his body going slack again, drifting back into sleep. She kept her arms around him, even though the bottom one, her right, began to ache. The smell of the burrow was alive in her nostrils, the mustiness and the smell of Peter. And she felt defeated. Because she could not leave him. She couldn't give him up. All of the strength she'd always felt had gone into her arms so that she could hold Peter better. There was no getting it back from him.

She watched him dream, and after a while, she slept. But, in case the pirates came in the night, I kept my eyes on the doorway. Me, and a hundred wooden birds.

TWENTY-NINE

There were small signs that the dry season was approaching. Certain patches of trees held leaves just going brown at the edges. Afternoon showers—which were common even well into the hot season—seemed to be dissipating. Tiger Lily noticed these small signals, as all Sky Eaters did. But she noticed them with a feeling of dread. As soon as the afternoon rains let up completely, there would be a relentless dry heat on the island. The villagers would look at the sun and the moon and the trees and announce that without a doubt the dry season had arrived. And then she would be married.

The mood in the village these days was foreign to her. It seemed to have happened without her noticing, and it emphasized how far away her attention had been for so long.

Because rather than show up at Tik Tok's door looking for advice and medicine, the villagers now gathered at Phillip's door. Some of them had even adopted the same loving but pitying glance when they looked at Tik Tok, as if they weren't quite sure he was living as nature had intended. Even Aunt Sticky Feet was overheard asking the other women why he was being so stubborn. She wanted Tik Tok to go to heaven, too, where there was always someone to build your fire for you, where you never had to sew, and where fish and meat cooked themselves. Tiger Lily wondered how much of this she had heard from Phillip, and how much she had conjured herself. Aunt Sticky Feet was known to have a vivid imagination.

Tiger Lily found Tik Tok one morning sitting in his house when all the elders were gathered at the fire.

"Why aren't you with the council?" she asked.

He was mixing herbs, and he moved his hands expertly even as he spoke. "I was uninvited."

"Why?" she asked, surprised.

Tik Tok filled pouch after pouch with his herb mixture. "Phillip says when I'm ready to do the right thing, I can come."

The thought of Giant being at the council fire, with all his idiocy, and Tik Tok being excluded, was too strange to be real. "What does that mean?" she asked.

Tik Tok looked at her deeply.

"They'll get past it," she said. "Once they think it through, they'll realize they need you."

Tik Tok was silent, like he wasn't sure. She'd never seen him truly unsure of anything.

That evening at the burrow she arrived to a beautiful sight: the trees had been festooned with candles. The twins were hauling bundles and boards up into the high limbs. Peter was directing it all while carrying Baby under one arm and making funny faces at him. The sight of him holding Baby always seemed like it fit and didn't fit at the same time.

He smiled up at her; clearly he'd heard her coming.

"What's this?" she asked.

"We're sleeping in the trees tonight. I thought you'd like it." She smiled, and Peter seemed pleased with himself.

"The twins are in charge of our bed. I've got to make sure they're doing it right, though. Hold this." He dropped Baby into her hands and shinnied up the tree quick as a monkey.

She stared at Baby, but he didn't cry. He was warm and soft. And though she knew she wasn't holding him quite right, she had gotten used to him enough that it was nice feeling his little squirming body in her hands.

As the dusk deepened, they gathered up their food and drinks and games and ascended into the trees, climbing limb to limb. They were so high they could see the shadow of Bear Mountain silhouetted against the last light of the setting sun. The air smelled of pine needles and oak. I kept glancing down at the forest below, but I had begun to relax.

The boys and Tiger Lily stayed up late playing cards. Tiger Lily had never played, and Slightly taught her the rules. She beat them three out of four times.

"Are you ever going to come live with us?" Tootles asked.

Tiger Lily looked down quickly to avoid his eyes. "I don't know." She didn't look at Peter.

Afterward, the boys separated to their treetop beds, and Peter and Tiger Lily curled onto their platform, wrapped up in thin suede blankets. They lay on their backs and the sky showed itself to them, the stars limitless.

Tiger Lily reached out and touched a leaf above them, to reassure herself it wasn't dry. It was supple to the touch.

Whatever always troubled Peter in his sleep, it seemed a million miles away from him now. He lay his arm out as a pillow for her head, while his was against the hard board. He made sure every bit of her was covered with blanket. He held tight to her waist with his free hand.

"I'm too mixed up for you," Peter finally said; it came out of nothing but silence. "That's what you think."

Tiger Lily looked at him. "Peter, no."

He gazed at her intently, and he seemed adrift. "You'll never come to stay with us, forever?"

She was silent. Tiger Lily's head was full of thoughts, of Tik Tok and Pine Sap and Peter and Giant, and how none of it fit together. After a while, with silence between them, Peter drifted off to sleep. It was a long time before she followed him.

It was I who woke up first.

Below, a shadow was approaching in the night, slowly, through the bushes. As it moved closer, it resolved itself into separate figures—ten altogether. Grown men. Pirates.

Beside me, I felt Tiger Lily come awake. Her skin prickled against me and her belly caught fire with fear. An instinct made her draw her hand to her waist for her hatchet, which wasn't there. She'd left it at the bottom of the tree, after trimming some branches for one of their games. She felt Peter's arm shoot over the top of her to contain her.

My thoughts immediately went to the other boys. Would Tootles scream if he woke to see the pirates? Would Baby cry?

I followed Tiger Lily's gaze as she silently turned her head to the right. In the trees closest to them, Nibs was awake, his eyes glinting at her in the moonlight.

The pirates circled the burrow, stood above it. Smee and another man knelt beside the tree stump, working at something quietly. Sparks began to issue from their hands. They lit several tiny flames, at different edges of the stump. The flames caught. Smoke began to rise from the burrow. Beside us, Peter's body was stiff and tensed, ready to fight. Tiger Lily's heart was pounding. Peter and she might be a match against many of the men. But the other boys wouldn't. If they fought, the boys would be easy targets.

*   *   *

The pyre grew. It was a breezy night—perhaps the pirates had planned it that way—and the flames fanned into the air. They stood with their daggers and cutlasses out, waiting for the boys to emerge. What would happen when they didn't and the pirates began to look for them?

The smoke made me dizzy. I began to sway. I felt Tiger Lily's hands sweeping me against her beating heart.

Only Smee didn't watch the flames. He was examining the ground.

Nibs must have managed to silence the other boys, because there was no sound from them. I waited to hear Baby's cry, knew it would happen at any minute and they would be defenseless.

In the firelight, I could see Hook's back. He was all bones, and in the strange shadows I noticed for the first time that he looked almost starved. I could see him start to slump in confusion as no one came out of the burrow, his body become concave in a question, and then tenser, angrier.

While the others were staring at the smoking hole in the ground, still catching on, Hook's head swiveled, and he seemed to look right at us in the trees. I was burrowed against the suede of Tiger Lily's tunic, and it seemed to me that the sound of my wings brushing against each other was deafeningly loud. It seemed that we must be completely visible—big, dark, still lumps in the softly swaying trees.

But there was no telling, because Hook looked away. Was it a trap?

We must have stayed like that for half an hour or more.

As the burrow lay in cinders, two of the men crawled in to search it, coughing. When they emerged shaking their heads, Hook whispered to the men, and they spread out.

They walked right underneath us. Across the darkness, Nibs and Tiger Lily locked eyes; his were terrified.

And then, below, Smee stopped at the foot of our tree. He was studying Tiger Lily's hatchet. He picked it up, ran his hand along the handle, and laid it down again. He didn't look up from the ground.

Our luck was that Hook, Smee, and the others didn't wait until morning for us to come back from wherever they thought we might be. In the light of day, we would have been impossible to miss. Maybe the pirates thought we were trapping them, and wanted to get away before they were caught.

They trailed away, watching their backs as they retreated in the direction they'd come. Long after they were gone, Tiger Lily and the lost boys stayed up in the trees, until dawn began to make out their figures to each other. The light reminded them they were still alive.

They climbed down warily.

From near the burrow, I heard Peter's harsh, angry laughter. He was making jokes about the pirates' eyesight, saying that Hook couldn't get at them even when they were right above their noses.

But the laughter was broken. Peter's face was ashen. And the burrow lay in smoking rubble.

It was easy to guess the route the pirates were taking home. I wanted to make sure they were on their way out.

To my relief, I found them making a beeline for the cove. Smee, as usual, hung at the back.

I was too far behind them to see what summoned him to the water at first. But to my surprise, there was Maeryn, reaching her hand up to him from the water's edge.

For a moment I was sure she would drown him. I hoped that she would. But then she simply handed him something I couldn't see. And before he could process it, she had sunk under the water again. Smee held the object in his hands, staring at it, and I flew close enough to see it was a whistle. Her voice echoed in his ears, telling him to use it if he wanted to call her to the shore.

What Maeryn could want with Smee, I could only guess.

Tiger Lily was late getting home. Giant was waiting for her in her hut when she got there. She froze in her tracks. Giant looked her up and down. He stank of clove oil and pipe smoke, and while Tiger Lily was not small, standing at his full height, he dwarfed her.

"Where were you?" he asked, sucking on his teeth, anger in his dull eyes.

Tiger Lily's gaze flitted to his. "Hunting. I was tracking an okapi I wounded. I lost it."

Giant took this in unsteadily. His eyes were watery and dazed from caapi water. He was drunk. "If you lie to me, I'll kill you," he said. "You sneak. I know you do."

Tiger Lily met his gaze more directly now. "I'm not lying."

He swayed on his feet a little. "No more sneaking," he said.

Giant's hands were enormous. He reached for her neck. Tiger Lily felt his fingers against her collarbone, and tried not to shudder. His breath hit her face, over and over. "My wife," he said. Then, he let go, and sank down onto her bed. "I could kill you," he muttered, then lay down on his side. First he propped himself on one elbow, trying to get the room into focus. But in another moment, he let himself give in to gravity. His eyes closed as he passed out.

THIRTY

Peter said he hadn't been careful enough, and that he had put the boys in danger. But all of the boys insisted that wasn't true. He began looking for a new hiding place, and settled on a spot up and across the river, beyond a patch of briary undergrowth that seemed almost impassable, and began to build. After fearing for their safety for so long, I was relieved to see them move. They tried to make it as much like the old burrow as possible. Almost as if they could pretend that nothing had ever happened.

Tiger Lily stayed home for a few days, longer than she had in some time. Giant wouldn't allow her to do otherwise. She knew that Peter would be hurt, and she planned to get away as soon as she could, but so far, the opportunity hadn't come.

She helped Tik Tok pack one afternoon. He was going to

a meeting of the shamans. This meeting took place twice a year, in the village of the Bog Dwellers, and was very mysterious. And she could tell he was relieved to get away.

"Watch my house, little beast?" he asked, putting the last things into his leather bag.

She nodded.

He bent and kissed her on the forehead. "When I come back, we only have days until your wedding. Please save some of them for me," he said. "I want us to have some time away like before, just the two of us. We can pretend nothing is changing."

Tiger Lily nodded again at his sad smile.

Tik Tok ambled out the door, clanging and weighed down with all of his potions and the recipes he intended to share. He took the path toward the river, and would meet the other shamans far downstream, a day's journey.

Tiger Lily sat after he left, listening to the sound of silence in his house. She thought about one word he'd said. *Days.* Only days.

Outside the air was getting drier. The forest was going brown and pulling in on itself.

She was to be married.

She listened to the silence and the *tick tick* of Tik Tok's clock. She turned to look at it.

At dusk in Neverland, as with anywhere else, all the colors begin to fade one by one before night comes. The last color to disappear is green, and in those moments between dusk and darkness, it stands out brightly for lack of all the other colors, and almost glows.

As Tiger Lily walked to meet Peter at the bridge so he could lead her to the new burrow, the world was this color of green. Green tall grass along the creek, green moss at the edge of the bridge. Green leaves over graying trees. She held the clock rolled gingerly in the folds of her tunic.

Peter stood on the bridge, elbows on the rail, looking over the water, into the mouths of the crocodiles below. He had a sadness that told itself through his whole body, the listless set of his arms, the slump of his delicate shoulders. But when he saw her coming, he straightened up and rallied, held his shoulders back and smiled as if there were nothing wrong at all.

She leaned next to him on the rail. He reached for her hand, but she reached for her stomach, and unrolled her tunic. She held the clock on to the rail, grasping it with both hands tightly.

"This," she said, "is time."

Peter stared at the clock in wonder. He reached out to touch the little silver hands, but Tiger Lily shook her head. "It's delicate," she said. "I just brought it to show you. I have to take it back."

He nodded. He leaned on his elbows on the rail beside it and watched with amazement as the seconds ticked by. He smiled, and this time his eyes twinkled.

"I think I believe it," he said. He put his hand on her cheek, tugged at a strand of her hair. "Thank you."

Just as he pulled back, there was a sound behind them in the bushes.

It was so close that Tiger Lily and Peter both jumped. Peter drew his knife. A figure stepped out of the bushes.

Pine Sap.

Tiger Lily stayed where she was, in the middle of the bridge, holding on to the clock protectively, as if she were a thief.

"I was looking for you," he said, his eyes big and slowly taking things in. "I followed your tracks," he stammered.

They looked at each other, and then Pine Sap swallowed, looked down at the clock in her arms.

She could see it all coming together in his head. She could see that he was seeing the lie. He looked at Peter, then at her.

"But you're going to be married," he said, still making it make sense.

Beside her, Peter stood perfectly still for a moment, and then he turned and ran away, disappearing into the woods.

Pine Sap stayed a moment longer than Peter did, not letting go of Tiger Lily's eyes with his wide, wounded ones. And then he, too, turned and walked in the opposite direction.

Tiger Lily, alone now, began to shake.

She leaned into the rail, looking at the water below, her hands trembling. The clock teetered for a moment on the edges of her fingers. She reached with her arms, tried to catch it with her wrists, but it bounced against them, slipped through the space between her hands. She watched in shock as it fell directly into the gaping jaws of the biggest crocodile. There was the loud snap of the animal's teeth. And then came the creature's realization that something was wrong. It whipped its tail from side to side, distressed, and slid off the muddy shelf into deeper water.

Just for a moment, she could hear the muffled *tick tick* from inside its mouth before it disappeared underneath the murky surface, and curled away.

THIRTY-ONE

She found Peter attempting to talk a jacamar out of its nest. He was trying to imitate its call.

"How long have you been here?" she asked.

"All day. I still can't get it right." His brow furrowed with concentration and frustration with himself. "Peter, get it right," he muttered.

"I thought you thought talking to the birds was stupid." Peter didn't reply. He kept on practicing.

She sat beside him, and he laid his hands on his lap, giving up for the moment. The sounds of the forest were gentle and quiet. Finally he seemed to really notice she was there and he put his arm around her and kissed her cheek.

"I needed to tell you," she said.

Peter looked at her. "Tell me?" Peter was the best at

pretending, of anyone I've ever seen, before or since. He smiled brightly and threw a rock at a tree for target practice, though there was uncertainty under his smile.

"Peter." Tiger Lily's voice shook. Her face went a deep red. "It was the truth. I'm going to be married."

Peter laughed; it bubbled out. And as soon as it did, it went still.

"You're joking." He smiled again. It was more of a grimace. "I'm not. . . ."

He pulled his arm away sharply.

"Your friend was lying and so are you. Why would you lie about that?"

He stood up. He stuck his hands into his pockets, softened.

"You're not going to do it, though," he said softly, as if it were a matter of course.

"It's what I've been sworn to do," she said. "Tik Tok promised."

Secretly, she wanted Peter to say no, and demand that it wouldn't happen. She wanted to tell him she needed him. He was silent.

"I'll be married in twelve days," she said, with finality.

"You're telling the truth?" he said flatly.

She nodded.

He looked up at the trees, as if tracking the birds from earlier.

"Peter," she whispered, pride rearing up. She suddenly wanted to put as much distance between them as possible.

"It was like, sometimes my life at home doesn't seem real. Sometimes I can't see myself when I'm with you. I can only just see you."

He stood up.

"You're worthless to me, Tiger Lily," he said.

He walked off into the woods. She sat on the ground, listening to the calls of the birds.

THIRTY-TWO

There were rumors of a ship spotted off the coast, gathered from some Bog Dwellers that Stone and some others had run into on a long hunt. Phillip went to the shore once a day to look for it, and kept claiming—half crazily, everyone decided—that they'd come for him at last. But Tiger Lily didn't really believe it, and neither she nor I really thought about it. She began the ten-day ritual of preparing for her wedding.

Weddings in the village were solemn affairs. Each day, she had to walk to the river with the other women and be washed from head to foot. Each woman gave her a gift, and these surprised her in their sincerity and thoughtfulness. From Moon Eye, of course, there was the long skirt, with the picture of the bird. But from Aunt Agda, there was a pair of slippers lined with fur. From Red Leaf, a shell necklace painted with a smiling crow. From Aunt Sticky Feet, a new necklace of fine turkey feathers. All painstakingly and lovingly made.

Tik Tok had returned, and she saw him one afternoon as she passed his house, looking around for the missing clock and muttering to himself. He didn't mention it to her, clearly sure he had misplaced it on his own. But he looked distressed, like it was weighing on him. Tiger Lily would go to hover at his door, planning to tell him, and then hesitate, unsure how to do so without telling him too many other things. So she waited, and tried to think of what to say. And she wondered when she had become the kind of person who wasn't brave enough to say the truth to him.

She didn't go on the walks with him that they'd planned before he'd left. She couldn't look him square in the face, so she kept avoiding it. And to be fair, he seemed so consumed by other matters that he didn't much pursue it either.

Each night, she lay in her bedroll, sleepless.

She imagined Peter appearing in different ways. She imagined him kneeling outside her house, listening to her breathe . . . standing on the edge of the forest, waiting for her to get up and come find him . . . padding down the village path at night barefoot, intent on entering her house and waking her with his hands, whispering that she should be quiet. Each of these possibilities seemed as real to her as the last, setting her skin on fire as she lay awake. But nothing changed. When she got up at night, when the moon was passing the middle of the sky, and she walked the perimeter of the village while everyone else slept, she saw no one.

She went to find Pine Sap one afternoon. He had been avoiding her, sitting at the other side of the circles at dinner, taking a different path when he saw her coming his way.

He was sanding the floors of his house smooth. He didn't look up at her as she approached and laid her hand on one of the poles, leaning slightly against it and watching him.

"I'm sorry I didn't tell you the truth," she said, standing with her hands folded in front of her, the closest to humility she could get.

She thought he would ignore her, but Pine Sap looked up.

"Are you leaving us for him?" he asked.

She looked at her feet. "No." She breathed. "I don't know."

Many things struggled on his face, anger being one of them. But hurt was the biggest. "You lied to me."

"I know."

He turned back to his work. "I always thought if you didn't have to marry Giant, you would have married me." His voice cracked. "I thought that was what you would have wanted."

Tiger Lily sank back in surprise. "But you'll marry Moon Eye."

He looked startled for a moment, and then recognition settled onto his face. He shook his head and laughed. "No."

"You built this house for her."

Pine Sap chewed on his bottom lip with a rueful smile,

and looked at her, disbelieving. "I built it for you," he said, amazed.

"But . . ."

"I know. It wasn't a rational thing. But I knew you'd like it. Close enough to home, but then, tucked away from everyone's eyes."

"But Giant . . ."

"Well, I was planning to poison him when I started." He smiled darkly, as if the idea was ridiculous now. "Then I just started hoping he'd let you have one thing you want. A wedding present."

Tiger Lily was silent. She couldn't feel worthy of the gift.

"Tiger Lily, you know Moon Eye isn't for me."

"She *is*," Tiger Lily said.

"She's *like* me. They're two different things. You're . . ." He swallowed. "You're everything to me. You know that. Don't pretend that you don't."

She wouldn't look at him. She knew, but she didn't want to know. More than anything, she worried for her friend. Because if it wasn't Moon Eye, no one was for Pine Sap. No one at all.

That night Tiger Lily sat up in the dark, unable to sleep. She counted the three days left of her free life to herself, over and over. The noises of the village had died for the evening and given way to the sounds of the forest, so active after dark with snakes and owls and other, deadlier night creatures.

Tiger Lily watched the sky from outside her house for a while. It seemed so low and warm, like she could reach out and touch its fabric. Finally she ducked back inside and stretched out on her bedroll, throwing an arm above her head and looking at nothing. Without the humidity of the wetter times of year, the air got cool after sundown. Her skin felt dry, and she worried her fingers against each other.

She must have fallen asleep, because she didn't hear him come in. When she did, he was kneeling right beside her head. She squinted at him in the dark, almost sure he was imaginary.

"Tiger Lily, I didn't mean it," he said.

Peter touched her hair with his hands, took strands between his fingers.

"Forgive me."

She'd never seen him so open and scared. His shoulders stooped, he looked smaller.

"You can come live with us. We can go farther away so we're never found. You can still be my wife."

He reached for her hand and squeezed it. "Please."

"I can't," she said. It was automatic.

"But you'll forgive me. I know you're angry but you'll forgive me. You can't live without me."

She sat up. "I can live without anyone."

Peter's breath came faster and harder. "I need you to say you'll come."

Everything tilted back and forth inside her. She felt

herself weaken and slump in surrender. She made her choice.

"I need two days to say good-bye," she said, feeling sick and also joyful. "I'll meet you at the bridge, midday, not tomorrow night but the next." She was struck by how little time it was. But it was all she had left.

Peter sat next to her. He wrapped his arms around her. He kissed her on her cheek, and on her lips. He gathered her hair up in his hands like he could take it with him.

"Okay, Tiger Lily. Okay."

He stood and left as silently as he'd come. She sat, legs wrapped in her covers. I felt her pulse slow down. But she couldn't sleep. She lay and watched the air turn gray with the morning light. She was awake to hear the first stirrings of people waking up. And then, finally, she drifted off.

THIRTY-THREE

T iger Lily was one of the last to discover what was happening that morning. Instinct must have told everyone to steer clear of her, to tiptoe past her, on their way to do what they'd convinced themselves wasn't a horror.

She was beveling a spear for Pine Sap, a parting gift. She had the tip in her sight line and was chipping away at the point. She hadn't turned her mind to leaving Tik Tok, because that would cause her to lose heart. And she hadn't noticed the village had gotten quiet around her. Nor had I, so wrapped up as I was in Tiger Lily's head. Her thoughts were far away, with the burrow. She only looked up from her work when she heard a collective murmur rise from the other end of the village.

Still, she didn't know anything was wrong at first. It was curiosity that pulled her down the path toward the square.

She couldn't see him right away. Her view was obscured by the crowd around him. But then, two people in front of her parted, and there he sat. He was wearing his raspberry dress. Phillip stood behind him. Tik Tok's face was still and empty. In fact, his expression was so foreign she almost didn't recognize him, despite the dress and the long, flowing hair.

He caught her eye; Phillip moved his hands behind him, and all at once she knew what was happening.

Phillip lifted Tik Tok's ponytail and began to saw at it with his knife. Tiger Lily lurched forward, but the crowd was slow to part, and by the time she reached the front, the ponytail had dropped to the ground with a soft *thwush*.

Phillip laid breeches of the standard brown leather that all the men wore on Tik Tok's lap. He smiled at Tik Tok.

"That wasn't so bad, was it?" he asked.

Tik Tok stared down at the clothes in his lap.

It was all over quickly. The crowd moved away. Only as it dissipated did people begin to mutter to one another about what had just occurred, with an air of uncertainty. Red Leaf doubled back and scooped up Tik Tok's ponytail to give it to him. No one seemed to understand what they had done to him.

Tik Tok sat alone, staring down at his feet, the same blank expression on his face. He looked like a stranger.

Phillip knelt next to him. "You'll be happier this way," he said warmly. "I promise you, Tik Tok. The women made the pants for you."

He glanced up at Tiger Lily, and she could only return disbelief on her face. No rage. Not yet. Phillip stood, patted Tik Tok on the shoulder, and walked off.

Tiger Lily took his place by Tik Tok's side, slid her hand into his, but his fingers didn't respond. Without his long hair, he looked smaller, older.

"What did they do?" she whispered. She heard a noise and turned to see Pine Sap, just arrived. Long strips of wood lay piled in his arms, and he stood still and surprised, his mouth open and catching air.

"H-help me," she stuttered.

They lifted Tik Tok by his armpits, and he didn't make it difficult for them. He stood and walked, cooperatively, but without moving to stand on his own. He let them lead him to his house, and put him into his bed, while Pine Sap ran to get a cup of hot water. Once he returned, Tiger Lily mixed some tea to soothe him, and as with the walking, Tik Tok merely cooperated and drank it in small, slow sips. She had the feeling that if she'd offered him a cup of worms to drink, he would have obeyed.

She covered him with his fur blanket. When she went to his trunk to find that it had been emptied, all of his beautiful dresses gone except the one he wore, the rage finally set in.

She found Pine Sap out by the central fire. He had taken

the men's clothes Phillip had given to Tik Tok, and was burning them, piece by piece, in the fire.

"You should have stopped this," he said.

"I got here too late. I didn't know. . . ."

"Before. You should have stopped it before. You are always somewhere else." He wasn't angry. Just disappointed. "You're his daughter."

She must still be getting older, she thought, because Tiger Lily felt something entirely new. She had never felt like a coward before.

She didn't notice the number of days going by, and she didn't go to meet Peter, so consumed was she in watching over Tik Tok.

He did not rally as the days went on. In fact, it was the opposite. He sank into himself and turned inward. He ate when Tiger Lily fed him, but it was clear that if she hadn't, he would have easily gone without. He did not come to tribal dinners, didn't wash himself or go into the woods. He stopped looking around distractedly for his clock. He did not take off his raspberry dress, and by the days it accumulated layer after layer of dirt. His hair became slick and greasy and wild, sticking up from his head in all directions. And most of all, he stopped talking. After the day his hair was cut, he did not say another word. He became mute, like me.

As shaman, Tik Tok was the only person who could marry Tiger Lily and Giant. Each day he remained in bed meant another day that the wedding was delayed. But this was only a vague consolation to Tiger Lily.

Her anxiety grew as the days went on. At first, she knew that he would have to recover. Then, she began to wonder *if.* She cast the thought out of her mind, because of course he would. But sometimes, when she sat watching him, she recognized that he was wearing someone else's face. And she didn't know if that was something you could come back from, because she had never seen it happen before.

Obsessively, she wondered what to do about the Englander. Her heart hardened more and more toward Phillip as the days passed, so that she couldn't see him without clenching her fists. Her heart went bitter and black whenever he crossed her mind.

One evening, when she was putting Tik Tok to bed, she was staring at that face, and suddenly she grabbed his hand, and tried to force her way toward him.

"Tik Tok, I have something to tell you. I have a secret. I took your clock," she whispered. He blinked at her, made no sign that he understood or cared. "I lost it at the bridge. I dropped it into the mouth of a crocodile by mistake, and now it swims around the island all day, telling the fish about time. It's gone."

Tik Tok didn't stir. He just blinked at her. "I'm sorry. I did it because I wanted to show it to someone. He lives in the woods and I go to see him. Tik Tok, I'm in love with Peter Pan."

If the shock of it reached him, he didn't show it. He didn't look worried, or angry, or surprised. And this sank her heart most of all.

And she didn't know, but all this time she was taking care of Tik Tok, she was letting Peter slip through her fingers. Because when she turned her attention to him again, everything had changed and couldn't be turned back.

THIRTY-FOUR

W hen I first heard of the Wendy bird, I didn't think any more about it. The words slipped past my ears. Neverland was full of creatures I'd never heard of.

I didn't connect it with the morning the warriors came running back from the hunt saying there was, indeed, a ship, and that this one had anchored safely off our shores.

The Sky Eaters, and Tiger Lily in particular, knew in an instant they had come for Phillip, just like he had said they would. And Tiger Lily thought fiercely that they couldn't take him away soon enough.

Several of the tribe members offered to join him on his journey to the ship, now that the aging disease had been deemed a thing that belonged only to the English and their strange continent. Phillip packed up some food and gifts from the tribe for the trek to the shore, and Tiger Lily watched him and the others walk out, and hoped he would never come back.

The ship had been anchored for a few days when she finally felt she could go find Peter. She made sure Tik Tok was fed and put in bed for the afternoon, though she knew Pine Sap and Moon Eye would be there to watch over him. She glared at anyone who looked at her on her way out.

Peter had explained to her where the new burrow was located, but it was still hidden enough that she had to backtrack a few times past landmarks before she found it. From there, she followed their tracks into a glade.

The boys were all in a clearing, laughing about something. To her surprise, even Peter was laughing. None of them ran to greet her. They were strangely off their guard.

It seemed odd that Peter had his back to her and kept it that way as she approached, though she knew what the reason must be: he had, no doubt, waited for her at the bridge, and she'd never come. But then, there was something strange about the way he held himself.

And then she saw, at the same time I did, that there was someone new among them. Chattering away to the boys, who were all raptly listening and laughing, she was so like Phillip's descriptions of heaven that for a minute I thought she was an angel.

She was perched on a rock, in a dress the color of a calla

lily, and with eyes even bluer than Peter's. Her hair was curly, and fell down her back and over her shoulders in a carefully arranged wave. Her skin was cloud-like with whiteness. Her mouth was an O as she looked at Tiger Lily, and then quick as a mouse, she slid off her rock and ran behind Peter, who turned to stand between her and whatever ghastly thing she'd seen.

When he saw who it was, his body relaxed, but his face went cold and blank.

"Oh, Wendy, it's our friend. Tiger Lily."

The girl's eyes appeared above his shoulder, then she slid out from behind him, gathering herself. She stepped forward and shook Tiger Lily's hand.

"I'm Wendy, pleased to meet you," she said.

She retreated back to her rock, climbed onto it again carefully, slipping many times as she did so, though it was only a small rock, and turned to eye her warily. Peter made no move to greet Tiger Lily.

Tiger Lily's eyes went to the stranger's neck. She was awed to see that the foreigner wore a necklace full of pearls just like her precious one, though Wendy's necklace must have held twenty of them.

The boys were all too shy around the visitor to say much of anything.

Finally, Nibs spoke up.

"This is the Wendy bird. We saw her up in a tree and thought she was a bird."

"One of the shipmates was showing me how to climb. We don't have many trees in the city. It was terrifying!"

"She fell on me," Curly said, in a voice near ecstasy.

I had always marveled at the femininity of some of the girls in Tiger Lily's village, but Wendy was a shocking contrast. Wendy bird was dainty in every way. Her arms and legs tapered into tiny wrists and ankles. Her chin was small and had a sweet little point to it. Her down-turned lower lip pulled her mouth into a soft, delicate frown, which she corrected by smiling often and at everything the boys said.

"I have to get back to the ship soon," she said. "They'll be worried."

"But you won't tell them about us," Peter said sharply.

"No, of course not. I'll say I got lost looking for shells."

Peter looked at Tiger Lily darkly, then absently threw a rock at a target behind her head, and it hit true.

Wendy gasped. "That's wonderful! How did you do that?" Peter looked surprised, smiled, then threw another one at the same target.

"Amazing!"

"You try, Wendy bird," Tootles said. And Peter nodded.

"Yes, your try."

Tiger Lily stepped out of the way. Wendy threw with a fragile, half-intended motion, and the pebble went flying far to the right of the tree. She laughed.

"Oh, I'm terrible." She looked over at Peter, and for the

first time something stirred in Tiger Lily. It was a feeling she didn't recognize.

Peter smiled and laughed and looked delighted. "I can teach you, next time you come."

Wendy lingered, though she kept saying she had to go. She laughed at everything the boys said that was even vaguely funny. She punctuated their stories with exclamations of support and admiration. And Peter looked like he didn't have a care in the world, so delighted did he seem with his visitor.

As the time wore on, Tiger Lily began to notice she was merely part of a rapt audience. Finally, she moved to leave.

When she said good-bye, the boys only muttered at her out of the sides of their faces, and I could see that many blushed as they looked at Wendy, and couldn't take their eyes off of her.

Well, she was one of the only girls they'd ever seen, Tiger Lily thought. Though they had never looked at her that way.

On the way home Tiger Lily talked with herself. The Wendy bird was beautiful, but she was not for Peter. She was a strange creature, another species—it was understandable that they were all fascinated. But Peter belonged to her.

She reassured herself in this way. And her noble nature wouldn't let her really believe Peter could ever betray her. But no matter what she said to herself, in the pit of her soul she feared the Wendy bird. From that first moment when she set eyes on her, the English girl scared her more than any other creature in the forest.

THIRTY-FIVE

Here is where I become more than an observer, and enter the story in my own right. Because I decided to return, to get another look at the Wendy bird and possibly regurgitate something on her head. And the moment I arrived back at the burrow, I felt the world go black a moment before I was pressed between two strong hands. It was Peter who'd caught me. How he'd memorized my flight habits, which of course were so fast I was virtually uncatchable, I never knew. "I want you to stay here," was all he said.

I've been called jealous. Vain. Cruel. Devious. Malicious. But let me say this: when Peter captured me and claimed me for his own, I stayed for one right reason, and one wrong one. The wrong one was that I was in love, and it was hard to say no to Peter. The right, and honestly, the bigger, reason was that I wanted to keep an eye on the Wendy bird for Tiger Lily's sake.

Peter started talking to me, where he had only ignored me before. He seemed to like my company, even though—or maybe because—I couldn't speak back. But I knew, by listening to his blood, that it was Tiger Lily swirling through his heart. He thought of her every time he looked at me. He waited for her, and I couldn't tell him why she didn't come. I'll admit, I hoped from time to time that her absence would turn his affections to me, now that he noticed I was alive. But in the end, it was neither Tiger Lily nor I who won Peter. Things don't work out as neatly as that.

I spent most of my time right next to Peter in those days. And so did Wendy. Her visits from the ship were an increasingly unwelcome part of my days.

She loved to sing on her visits, and she had a voice like a bird's. Whenever Peter was around, she straightened up and fidgeted with her face, moving her palms along her cheeks as if she could smooth her skin, toying with her blond, wavy bangs. Wendy's heart beat for Peter immediately—there was no slow growing, no dark distrustfulness like Tiger Lily had had, no hesitation. Wendy didn't believe in situations she couldn't bend to fit her, so there was no need to be distrustful. She had the blissful confidence of someone who had never been put in a pot of turkey broth to die.

Immediately, she loved Peter, just from looking at him. His wildness, his broken edges, were just things to be absorbed and loved, too.

I hated her, of course. And I had ways of letting her know. I tried to sting her at least once a day: no small feat, considering stinging can be quite painful and exhausting for a faerie. But it wasn't for lack of her merits that I detested her. For a girl who'd never known the woods, who'd grown up being comforted and pampered, she fearlessly threw herself into life at the burrow and caring for the boys. Where Tiger Lily saw the boys' boundaries and backed down, Wendy liked to brush them aside with a simple sweep of the hand. She assumed I was Peter's pet and that, because I didn't like her, I was jealous.

How Wendy made her way back to the burrow, time and again, through a forest that many found to be deadly, I have to chalk up to a matter of luck and blissful ignorance.

She had a certainty about her that was intoxicating. It was like she took the world and everything in it and compared it to her own rule book, and anything that was out of place was quickly dismissed, and anything that fit was more proof that her system was the right one. Her smile was never brighter than when she was being observed and found pretty.

As the boys were still in the process of putting the new burrow together, Wendy threw in her hat, assuming they'd be lost without her. The boys labored under her confident guidance. They placed doors where she insisted they should go. Tootles slapped his forehead as if seeing the light at times like this, and the twins fell over themselves with how smart her ideas were, and everyone pretended they couldn't have thought of any of it themselves.

Only Nibs seemed to be dubious of her, and I could see he was the only one who felt there might be a conflict of loyalty between exhausting themselves to please Wendy, and being true to Tiger Lily. But the other boys loved being bossed. For a group of boys who'd always taken pride in their independence, they seemed to love that Wendy wanted to mother them. And Peter, shockingly, loved it most of all.

He often turned to her, confused. "Where should I put this? What should I do here?"

Wendy flicked her finger here and there. And Peter smiled and obliged. It was like someone had figured out the answers for him to questions that had confused him for so long. The nights after Wendy visited, he slept like a log and didn't seem to dream at all.

For her own part, Wendy had read someone named Jane Austen. She knew romance. As she worked next to the boys, she liked to imagine herself in a novel. Peter was one of the brooding heroes, and she was the heroine, better than all other girls he had ever seen. That was how she got through the days of dirt and mud and bugs. And, of course, by knowing that it wouldn't be forever.

She wanted everyone asleep at the same time she was, two hours after sundown, because she was a morning person and liked to visit early, so the boys gave up their late nights. They loved to be muddy and messy; she forced them to swim in the river. She carried them soap from her ship, preciously cupped in the hem of her dresses.

"I have brothers on the ship, and they hate getting clean too, but it's a necessary evil."

She loved to be looked at, and groomed herself constantly. The woods didn't allow for her to ever be perfectly clean, but to the boys, she was pristine as springwater.

Peter liked to watch her, her curls and her lily-white skin. She interested and fascinated him. And the truth was, he wanted to forget Tiger Lily, and Wendy was a welcome thing to think about. But when he was in his bed, restless and howling inside, he thought only of Tiger Lily.

As you may have guessed already, Peter had a soul that was always telling itself lies. When he was frightened, his soul told itself, "I'm not frightened." And when something mattered that he couldn't control, Peter's soul told itself, "It doesn't matter." So while I trained my ears and tried to listen hard to him, I couldn't always make out where he was, or what he felt. And so each time he let Wendy come a little closer, I didn't see what it meant, or how it would end.

By the time I returned to the village for a visit, to see what was happening with Tiger Lily, a hoard of Englanders had returned with Phillip. To my surprise, rather than pulling him away, they had come trundling in . . . with their exotic gifts and their maps and their curiosity. The village was a flurry of activity.

Though Tiger Lily anticipated the day that they would turn around and leave, and take Phillip and all of his ideas with them, the Englanders appeared to have other intentions—and they'd taken to the village as if it were home. From the looks of the villagers—walking around trussed up in hats and scarves and beads—the Sky Eaters had greeted this idea with open arms. A few of the older women, including Aunt Sticky Feet, muttered and took to their houses distrustfully. But all in all, it was a celebration.

The talk, on the first few days, had been about departures. And now the talk was about how many people they planned to leave behind, to continue Phillip's work and learn more about the plants and the people, and what they could gain from them, and when they would send more ships back, and what a beautiful and exotic spot it would make for travelers and explorers.

I found Tiger Lily sitting by Tik Tok's side, in a haze of confusion and disappointment. She wondered if that day behind the waterfall, where all people were forbidden to go, she had angered the gods so much that they had left the village for good.

Tik Tok didn't seem to notice. But later, when everything had changed beyond repair, she wondered if he must have thought, like she did, that it was the end of their ways forever.

THIRTY-SIX

I followed Peter on solitary walks, when he traversed the edges of the area where the boys now hid and watched for pirate tracks.

We were out on one of these walks when Wendy appeared in our path. She looked like a fawn, startled and unsure.

She smiled. I didn't like the look of the smile. It was too confident of Peter.

"The boys told me I'd find you somewhere around here."

"Yeah."

Peter put his arms up against a bent tree, restless, but happy to see her.

"They're talking about when we'll depart," Wendy said. "I guess we'll leave some people behind. But of course, I'll be going."

Peter nodded, his arms still against the tree.

"Peter, do you ever think of leaving here?" she asked.

Peter shook his head. "Of course not."

Wendy seemed to be mustering her courage. "You could, you know. I could look after you." She looked scared. And for a brief moment of compassion, I realized she was just an uncertain human girl, like any girl. "I could love you," she said to the ground, her voice low with nerves.

Peter was silent for a few moments. He leaned harder against the tree; above his head, the branches swayed a bit. "You don't know me," he said. "I murder pirates. I take everything."

Wendy looked up and smiled with a trembling mouth. "No. You're wonderful."

Peter let out a long, slow breath. Wendy stepped closer. She kissed him, on the side of his mouth. He stood perfectly still. He didn't kiss her back. But he didn't move away either.

Later I understood.

Over those next days, I watched her and saw it clearly. When Peter made mistakes, Wendy cheered for him anyway. One afternoon he beat her and everyone else in a race organized by Slightly. She only laughed and squeezed his wrist with easy affection and told him how fast he was. She was so undeterred by losing that it made the boys wonder if winning was exactly what they'd thought it was or if in England it was different.

When Peter got angry with Slightly later that night, Wendy sat beside him at the fire afterward and offered her support.

"It's hard to be in charge," she said. "They could make it easier on you." I sat on the log beside her and thought about pulling out each one of her hairs, even her eyelashes. Of course, what she said was true, but it was something Tiger Lily never would have said. Tiger Lily didn't know how to be encouraging. And I hated that Wendy did, and Peter seemed to relax beside her.

Wendy made it clear, from that first day she arrived, that she could never walk away from Peter, and I suppose this had an effect too. She applauded him, and always sparkled in her eyes when she looked at him. She was like a bandage on his heart, and she tried to be the best bandage she could be, though what she was trying to help him heal from, she wasn't sure of. And every time she did something nice for him, his anger would say to him that Tiger Lily would never do something like that. Even his thoughts got clearer around her, and easier to read.

I began to see that Wendy had something Tiger Lily hadn't even known she was supposed to have. Of all the things Tiger Lily had thought she might have to be for Peter—strong, brave; to be big and to keep up—she had never thought that the one thing he wanted most from her was simply to show that she believed in him, always and without fail. For Peter, who feared losing so much, this was a great comfort indeed.

After several more days, he didn't move down the log when Wendy sat beside him. He got protective, so that when I tried to put dead bugs in Wendy's hair, or put poison ivy down on the places she loved to dangle her calves, he swatted me away.

And then one afternoon, when they were on a walk, with me lugging a tiny piece of pollen to stick in Wendy's nose, with a plan of inducing a large quantity of mucus to appear, she kissed him, and for a moment or two, he kissed her back. This sent Peter's head into another swirl, and Tiger Lily reared up in his heart and all around him. I dropped my pollen.

Maybe it would have been better to stay. But I saw the writing on the wall, even before Peter did. And I couldn't watch it happen. I made a bunch of useless, angry gestures at them both before I left, but they didn't bother to try to interpret them. I heard Wendy saying behind me that I was going off in a huff, and it made me sound small, and petty, and pointless. But the truth was, I was choosing. I was going where I belonged.

I am glad I was with Tiger Lily that afternoon, when she walked into Tik Tok's house and saw he wasn't in his bed. She thought it was a good sign, that he must be up and out in the village or in the woods on his own, and her heart lifted.

But he was not out in the village, and he did not come back from the woods.

She and Pine Sap followed his tracks. They led to the edge of the river, and went in.

He'd left his raspberry dress on the bank.

THIRTY-SEVEN

S he didn't remember running to Peter's. I tried to stop her from going. I flew in front of her eyes, I fluttered a wing into her nostril, I bit her on the shoulder. She didn't swerve once. Her feet took her to a circular clearing near the glade.

Only one figure was there, perched on a rock, weaving something between her fingers.

Wendy smiled when she saw her, but nervously, as if she still considered Tiger Lily a wild animal.

"Welcome," she said, like the clearing was hers and she was inviting her in. "You look awful. Is everything okay?"

Tiger Lily drifted down underneath herself. This was her one gift more than any other. Silently, she nodded. "Yes. Everything is okay."

"The boys are out hunting," Wendy said, looking around as if she needed their protection. The tiny tip of her nose dimpled when she smiled. "I just let them go without me. Peter is doing some thinking. And the best thing is to give them space."

Tiger Lily nodded again, though she did not know what Wendy meant.

Wendy seemed uncomfortable with Tiger Lily in the clearing. "Why don't you and I take a walk?"

"Okay."

Wendy marveled at the tiniest things as they wound through the woods.

Pointing to a poisonous spiky tree, she said, "How wonderful!"

Or, looking at Tiger Lily's bracelets, she said, "Oh, aren't you lucky! They're so unique!"

Mentioning that she'd heard about the wolf pup that Tiger Lily had given to Moon Eye, she exclaimed, "I've always wanted a wolf pup! She must love him so much! Can you get me one?"

She held her skirts against her legs as they walked, making sure to slowly avoid this tiny briar and that muddy boggy spot, for out of all the things in the forest, she noticed her dress the most.

They came to a creek, and here Wendy made them turn around.

"I can't swim," she explained. "I might get swept away."

Tiger Lily thought of Tik Tok, and for a moment, she wanted to sit down, right there in the middle of the path. But she straightened again as Wendy spoke.

"You'll miss Peter, I'm sure, if he comes with us. I don't know if the boys will come too. I hope you won't be too mad at me, to steal your friends like this. But believe me, it's for a good cause."

Tiger Lily tried to process her words. Go to England? Peter?

And it made Tiger Lily float above herself, feel outside herself. Because, wasn't Peter hers? Wasn't it her hand that always held Peter's? How else could it make sense?

"He says he has to think." Wendy suddenly looked at her anew. "Maybe you should come too. Everyone would love you. You're not conventionally pretty, but that's all right. You're exotic. I live in a beautiful house, it's a big yellow one, right on Finsbury Circus. We're an unconventional family," she said with pride. "You could stay with us. You'd love it." It was so out of Wendy's realm of imaginings that Peter could love Tiger Lily that she wanted to include her. She wanted to sweep them both up in her confident happiness. But Tiger Lily was only quiet in return.

"Will you tell Peter something for me?" she said finally.

Wendy nodded brightly.

"Will you tell him that my father has drowned?"

Wendy went still and white, and Tiger Lily nodded a good-bye, then turned and set a path for home.

* * *

In all of this there was one bright spot. In the village, the wedding had been pushed back one cycle of the moon, out of respect for the dead.

——————

THIRTY-EIGHT

T iger Lily's feet took her to the lagoon. She didn't plan it, it just happened. I trailed along behind her helplessly. I hovered near her cheek to watch for any tears I could catch for her. But of course, her eyes stayed dry.

She sat on a rock. She looked at the space where they had had the dance. She watched for the jellyfish under the water. She had the half-crazy, dazed notion that she could move herself back to another evening just by sitting in the same spot.

She wasn't paying attention to anything around her; she was moving inside her own endless space. So it took her several moments to see a pair of eyes watching her, just above the surface of the lagoon. Seeing Tiger Lily notice her, Maeryn raised her nose and mouth and chin from beneath the water and swam closer toward her. She smiled. The smile sent shivers through me, and set off every warning bell in my head. I couldn't see the shape of what she was planning, but I knew she was no friend. I huddled against Tiger Lily's neck, because though Maeryn's thoughts were too murky to hear, when her eyes flickered to me, she seemed to know what I knew. She seemed to know everything.

"You need me," the mermaid said, turning her eyes on Tiger Lily. "I guessed you would."

Maeryn propped herself onto her elbows in the muddy shallow water. Even in Tiger Lily's grief, Maeryn's beauty awed her. Maeryn gave her a searching, knowing look.

"The water swallowed your father. The fish saw it happen." The words rattled around in Tiger Lily's chest, which seemed to be newly hollow. "And Peter has betrayed you in your moment of need. Am I right?" Maeryn looked at her inquisitively, playing with a tendril of her wet hair and raking a piece of seaweed out of it with her fingertips.

Tiger Lily pulled her knees up to her chin and hugged them. It seemed to be all the answer Maeryn needed.

The mermaid shook her head. "It's in his nature, like I said. Peter will always be slippery." She sighed, and reached out to touch one of Tiger Lily's toes. Though Tiger Lily knew better, she let the mermaid do it. I feared she might drown her, but Maeryn merely stroked her foot, lulling her. "The Wendy girl can't stay." She turned her murky green eyes to Tiger Lily's face, considerately. I was the only one who saw the envy there. Tiger Lily merely shook her head, vaguely agreeing . . . though she probably would have agreed with any statement said by anyone at that moment.

Maeryn pulled her fingers away and dug a shell out of the mud, studying it. "I have a friend who wants the same things you do," she murmured, glancing up from the shell. "I can introduce you, if you like. Though I think you may have met briefly before."

Tiger Lily didn't answer. I knew the name before Maeryn said it. I flew up to Tiger Lily's ear and perched on her earlobe. I felt like I was on fire with the weight of what I knew and couldn't say.

"His name is Reginald Smee," Maeryn said.

I bit Tiger Lily, as hard as I could. I don't know how I thought it would help. Faerie bites are worse than wasp stings—they pierce and burn and ache all at the same time. At best, I knew, I'd be swatted away, and at worst she might crush me by accident in her sudden reaction to the pain. But what happened was worse. She didn't even seem to notice it at all. It was like Tiger Lily herself wasn't even really there.

"He'll wait for your fire, up on the plateau, every night at dusk until he sees it."

For a moment, Maeryn's eyes flicked to me. I could see in that one look that she saw my alarm, and it amused her. Tiger Lily stood up to leave, and all I could do was follow.

She didn't go to Reginald Smee that night. Instead, she woke Pine Sap from his spot on the floor of his house, late. In his sleep, the first thing he did was hug her. He held her tight, despite her stillness, despite her body never softening into his. He knew her well enough to know he needed to hold her anyway.

"I need help," she said.

In the morning, in the comfortable shelters the tribe had given to them, the visitors woke with an inkling that something was off. I happened to be in Phillip's tent at first light, scouring for dust mites.

He sat up in bed, and saw the feather lying on his blanket, just on top of his chest. He turned it around and around in his hand, curious, startled that it could have arrived in the night without him knowing it. And then he heard the scratching on the roof.

Some of the others had already come outside.

No one screamed. But one man fainted. I had to stay well hidden, but through the cracks of his shelter, I watched.

There were so many crows. Crows on the roofs. Crows on the path. Crows perched on every bare surface, so that all the paths through the village were black instead of brown.

The villagers began to mutter to each other. They knew what it meant, even if the Englanders didn't.

They were sure—even before they saw her, standing in the square, her hair cut as short as Tik Tok's had been—what it meant. Their gods were back. Tiger Lily had called them. And the Englanders were doomed.

THIRTY-NINE

T he Tiger Lily I knew had disappeared. I listened and listened and heard nothing inside her. I don't know where she went during those days. But her body remained and did things I couldn't predict.

I followed her one night into the dark forest, setting a path for the plateau. I felt her tremble. I thought she was scared of things she couldn't see. But later, I realized, she was scared of herself.

What could I do? I threw acorns into her water jug, stuck leaf stems in her ears, shoved a jagged pebble into her nostril, all to get her attention. But nothing slowed her steady pace. For the first time, I thought about going back to my swamp after all. I wanted to be somewhere where I didn't have to watch.

Up on the plateau, she lit a fire and waited, her back against a boulder, and far below in the darkness we could see the lights of tiny fires, all of different settlements across the island: her own village, and even the distant fires of the Cliff Dwellers. The lights would have been comforting on another night, but knowing what we were there for kept me on edge. Tiger Lily waited, her hand near her knife, dull eyed and still. I listened to her heart but it was a black pit; it sounded like the sky at night when it was too cloudy to see the stars.

The woods below were quiet. Animals had retreated into their burrows. The whole world seemed to be sleeping. Back home, I thought with sudden longing, the faeries would be gathered around a warm sulfurous spring, lounging and huddled together.

It must have been hours before we heard the sound of a pair of feet climbing up the last rise.

Smee appeared on the edge of a jagged, rocky area at the side of the meadow. His eyes flicked to Tiger Lily's knife as he approached. She watched him, expressionless. When he reached the circle of the fire, he crouched across from her and stirred a stick in the flames.

"You're willing to help us?" he said.

"Yes," Tiger Lily said, without hesitating.

"Bad things may happen to them." As he said this, visions of strangling Tiger Lily played in his head. He was tempted to lunge for her now, but he knew if he did, he'd be a dead man. Better to wait until the moment she was off her guard, when the time came. "You know that, don't you?"

Tiger Lily nodded. Her eyes were trained on the fire. "You promise me they'll happen to the girl, too?"

Smee nodded. Even he could see something had changed in her. He studied her face, and none of the fierceness and compassion he'd seen and admired was there. She was cold and empty. He wondered if maybe she wasn't worth killing after all.

Then suddenly, a flicker of the old Tiger Lily appeared, just for a moment. "But none of the boys. Only Peter and Wendy. Anyone else, and . . ." She gave him a warning look. She didn't have to finish.

Smee swallowed deeply, visibly afraid. But also, though Tiger Lily didn't see it, eager.

She drew a map for him in the dirt, tracing it all with a steady finger. Of course, Smee already knew the lagoon.

"We'll need you for bait," Smee said. If Tiger Lily had been more herself, she might have sensed the trap. But she only nodded, agreeing. Peter had abandoned her, but she knew he wouldn't abandon her to die.

She didn't see how intently Smee studied her face in the firelight. "They can't swim," she said finally. It was enough.

They arranged when and where they would meet. And then Smee turned and trudged back down the mountain, breathing heavily from the exertion. She watched him go, then sat in silence, listening to the crackle of the fire.

As Tiger Lily walked home, I pricked at her, I stung her, I pulled out several of her hairs. But she flicked me away easily. Still, I kept on trying.

Because there were two things I knew. Neither of us could ever really see Peter drowned and survive it. And it wasn't Peter that Smee planned to destroy.

FORTY

"They say there are pearls at Whitestone Beach."

Tiger Lily was standing amid the boys at the new burrow. Peter and Wendy had gone for a walk. They wanted all of the alone time they could get, Tootles said, while Nibs gave him an exasperated look. Of all of them, Nibs was the only one who really understood. From a tangle of bushes, Tiger Lily herself had watched them leave, their hands entwined, her heart cold as stone.

"Your hair," Slightly said. "It's . . . it's horrible." Nibs elbowed him, but Slightly's eyes were glued to Tiger Lily's scalp. "Did it catch on fire or something?"

"Why would we want pearls?" one of the twins asked. He was bouncing Baby on his knee. In the many months that she had known them, she realized, Baby did not seem to have gotten any bigger. Was he stuck in infancy forever?

"To make a gift for the Wendy bird," Tiger Lily said. "She loves pearls, didn't you notice?" Only Nibs looked suspicious. "She might be so grateful she'll take you to England with her."

The boys all shrugged. "Okay," said Curly, unable to resist rushing into anything that seemed vaguely foreboding.

I tried to get in their way, but of course they dismissed me. Slightly said I was having "lady's hysterics." One of the twins mentioned something he'd heard about women going crazy twelve times a year. Nibs pointed out that that was impossible since I wasn't a lady, and that insects were just irrational and you could never know why they did the things they did.

Tiger Lily led them through the forest, to where the path changed from dirt to loamy mud, trailing through scrubby little bushes that were spaced enough to leave natural footpaths. Finally, they reached the shore. This was a quiet inlet; the sand white and warm. And indeed, the ground just below the waterline was covered by beds of thousands of oysters.

They secreted Baby in a basket in the bushes, and waded in the water. Immediately, Tiger Lily plucked off her necklace and dropped it into the water, where it would probably never be found.

For many reasons, her one pearl no longer seemed as beautiful as it once had.

The boys hauled their oysters into the shade to shuck, sand stuck to their feet and calves. Never was there a group more relaxed, and happy to have something new to do.

Tiger Lily had brought two jugs of caapi water, packing them in on her back, and now as they sat in the shade of a palm tree, she offered it around. I sat on the bottle and tried to sting anyone who handled it, but they brushed me aside.

Tootles drank first. Then Slightly. Nibs looked suspicious, but took a sip. They all sat and talked and waited for the effects of the water to set in.

"I feel weird," Slightly said, and grinned.

"I feel fine," Tootles said solemnly. "But it's crazy that that tree's smiling at me."

"You're a real piece of work, Tootles," Nibs said.

"Don't say *work*," one of the twins said. "Bite your tongue."

Tiger Lily let their every word tattoo itself on her. Tomorrow, she would be a stranger to them; they would hate her. She knew this in a vague, distant way, as if she were watching herself from above, with no power to change things.

Finally Tootles slumped back and yawned. The others soon followed. The boys talked and fell asleep, one by one, until every last one of them was peacefully passed out in the shade, the soft lapping of the water lulling them. When she was sure they were all asleep, Tiger Lily stood quietly. She was tempted to forget everything and stay on the beach all day, until they woke up, and laugh with them like she used to. She had the sudden urge to kiss each one's cheek, but the gesture would have been too strange to her. She only patted Nibs's hand, as affectionately as she could, before she stood and walked back into the forest.

FORTY-ONE

She met the pirates at the edge of the lagoon. Maeryn was there, sunning herself on a rock in the middle of the water. The Never bird, perched on its enormous nest, watched them nervously and then lifted off, its giant wings flapping loudly. It perched itself on one of the low limbs hanging over the lagoon.

Hook was sitting on the beach. He stood when he saw her, holding his back and wincing, then smiled. It was a painful smile, with so few teeth. He looked desperate and wounded—like someone should be looking after him. She narrowed her eyes as she studied him. She seemed to doubt, for a moment, that he could really be the Hook Peter was so afraid of. But then, there was the unhinged quality to his eyes. As a hunter, she must have been reassured. His eyes hinted that he could be deadly in the same way a rabid possum could. He made no reference to her strange haircut, so uncharacteristic for a girl. He barely seemed to notice.

"It's simple, really," he explained. "We're just using the tides. We'll put you on the rock." He gestured to the rock where Maeryn now perched. "Peter will come to retrieve you. We'll ensure he'll be able to get out there, but not get back. The girl will be easy to grab." Hook was happy with the plan. It was simple, and clean. He would never even have to touch Peter. No matter what some of the men believed, he didn't long to feel his hands around the boy's neck. He just wanted him gone.

Hook had sent Mullins to lure Peter away from the new burrow. The men had all argued over who would have to do it. He was to allow himself to be caught, and confess— seemingly as a random aside—that Tiger Lily had been captured. The men, Hook explained, had drawn straws to determine who would have to go, because there was always the likelihood that Pan would kill the man immediately. But in the end Hook had picked the best liar.

They sat down on the beach side by side, Tiger Lily with her hand on her dagger, Hook propped up awkwardly with his hand rubbing at his lower back, and waited. I sat on the ground, my legs on the cool dirt, shivering. Tiger Lily observed, looking sideways, the swollen lump where his hand used to be. She noticed that his feet jerked back and forth with habitual tension, as if he were tapping them on the floor. This was a man who needed to crawl out of his own skin.

"Well, it should be soon, if they're coming," he said, almost resigned. He handed her a coil of rope. "Better be off."

Tiger Lily's heart kept a slow, steady pace, though mine began to race. She stood and walked into the murky lagoon water. Maeryn had promised her safety, but there was always the chance she would break her word and try to drown Tiger Lily on her swim. Tiger Lily was beyond caring. She swam out to the rock in the middle of the water with no incident, and scrambled onto it, sitting cross-legged. She shivered as she pulled the ropes around herself to make them look like they bound her arms and legs.

She waited.

I alighted on a craggy tooth of the rock and watched the woods like she did, hoping no one would come. The trees were silent for what seemed like forever, except for the usual sounds of birds and ground creatures. I wondered if Mullins was, indeed, dead. And then there was the quietest shuffle in the brush. Another moment, and a flash of brown. And then two hands parting the green of the bushes, and Peter, staring at Tiger Lily across the water, and moments later, the whiteness of Wendy behind him.

A canoe had been left on the opposite shore, meant to look as if the pirates had beached it there after they'd tied Tiger Lily. Peter's instinct must have told him that it was too obvious, but he didn't hesitate. He crouched his way along the tree line, quietly trying to push Wendy back to safety every few feet, with Wendy quietly insisting on following. She didn't know she was making things harder for him rather than easier. She was caught up in her own bravery.

I looked back at Tiger Lily, then skimmed just inches above the water to the shore. I stung Peter's hands as he handled the boat. Wendy swatted me away. "She hates me," she whispered, seeming to think that the focus of my entire life was trained on her.

I knew too well by now that they wouldn't listen to me, and it paralyzed me with sadness. I landed on the bow of the boat, exhausted, and watched helplessly as they paddled out, Peter signaling to Tiger Lily with his hands and looking around for signs of the pirates who, by all appearances, seemed to have abandoned her to the rising tide.

They reached the rock, and Peter climbed out to untie her. For a moment he met her eyes. But quickly, he swiveled to help Wendy out of the boat so that she wouldn't tip into the water without him to balance her. She crouched on the rock, and he told her to hold on to the boat's tip as he turned to Tiger Lily. I floated down onto a dead leaf.

It was at that moment that Tiger Lily let her ropes fall. She slid into the water like an eel. At the same moment, the boat seemed to drift out of Wendy's grasp of its own accord. No one saw the shadow of Maeryn's body underneath it, towing it away. To Wendy, the tide seemed to be carrying the boat in the opposite direction it was supposed to, out to the mouth of the lagoon and into the ocean beyond. But Peter wasn't looking. He was watching the place where Tiger Lily had disappeared underwater, trying to understand.

He was not afraid at first. He put his hands to his mouth and yelled for the mermaids.

He waited for a few minutes, and then called for them again. The water carried his voice clear and loud.

And then he waited. "They usually come right away," he said to Wendy, concerned but not fearful. He yelled again, Maeryn's name, then those of some of the other mermaids I didn't know. The water was strikingly silent.

And finally, recognition seemed to settle itself on his face, and a dawning fear. The last emotion to settle in was a sickening hurt. He knew in that one solid moment he had been betrayed.

I watched them from my leaf. There was nothing I could do now, even if they chose to notice me. At the other edge of the lagoon, I saw Tiger Lily emerge from the water and slide into the bushes silently, but Peter was looking in the other direction. He watched the water for several minutes, his face pale. All the life seemed to drain out of him. I began to lose my breath, clutching the leaf I was sitting on, flapping my wings together.

Wendy, up until now confident and unafraid, was studying him.

"Well, someone will come for us," she said. Because that was the way things always ended for people who were charmed. But Peter's silence said otherwise.

Peter didn't say that in an hour the tide would be in and the water would be over their heads, but she was reading it on his face. He looked from shore to shore, as if something might appear to help, though neither of them could imagine what. And Wendy, who was not stupid after all, began to shake, her breath becoming shallow.

"I can't die," she said. "I can't die."

Peter put his arm around her. "We won't die."

Tears threaded out of Wendy's eyes, though she was deathly silent.

I didn't want to watch, but I couldn't leave. The minutes passed. The water rose. The pirates had faded into the woods, maybe to watch in secret, as if Peter could still get at them even from where he was.

The water crept up the rock slowly but inevitably.

Peter was white as a ghost. It was the first time, outside of his dreams, I'd seen terror on his face. He held her arms to steady her, but his hands trembled violently. He studied the shore for Tiger Lily, or any sign of anyone, but other than me, they'd all vanished. His eyes lingered on me for only a second. I wondered if he realized then that I'd tried to warn him. But he finally just turned back to Wendy, and put his arms around her. He straightened himself up and seemed to try to grow to be more like a man.

She was silent. The tide seemed to move faster now. They shivered as it made its way up their bodies. Wendy lost her balance under the water for a moment and slid off the rock, but Peter managed to grab her and pull her upright.

She began to gasp, unable to calm herself enough to breathe.

The leaf I was sitting on became waterlogged enough to sink. I flew to shore, and perched on a berry bush. I thought I might be sick.

The sun was setting, obscured from view by the cliffs but sending slices of orange and purple into the sky at the horizon, though the darkness of the water swallowed the colors rather than reflecting them.

From where I sat, Peter and Wendy were the two loneliest figures in the world. But Peter was somehow the lonelier of the two.

FORTY-TWO

I t was soon dark enough that only the greens were glowing. And then they, too, dimmed as the darkness thickened.

I didn't hear her come up behind me. She was on her belly. I had given up on her. It didn't even occur to me to try to spur her into action. Whoever Tiger Lily was, she wasn't the person I knew anymore. For all I knew, she had sidled up beside me because she couldn't resist watching the spectacle of a drowning.

Across the water, Wendy seemed to be having some kind of choking fit. Peter was holding her hand, and his feet kept slipping. He was clumsy and dismantled, hunched over and desperate.

Tiger Lily moved so quietly I barely noticed until she was

already in the water.

She surfaced under the Never bird nest. From where I perched, I could just see her eyes glinting, and that her nostrils were above the water's dark surface.

From anywhere else, the nest would have looked to be simply floating. It seemed to move back and forth with the ripples of the water, so subtly that it was hard to tell that it was drifting toward the rock where Peter and Wendy were losing their footholds. I held my hands to my mouth, unsure what was happening, but hoping. Was this part of the plan she had negotiated with the pirates? It didn't seem like it could be.

The evening was so dark that Peter and Wendy were just shadows, and almost indistinguishable from the black water, but alert. Peter had seen the nest drifting toward him. I didn't dare go near, for fear of illuminating them with my glow and allowing any still lurking pirates to see.

Tiger Lily was halfway across the lagoon when I became certain she had changed her mind and that she was, indeed, going to save them.

I saw a fin just break the surface to her left, and I flew.

Before I was even close, Tiger Lily was yanked under the water.

There were three or four of them. Mermaids hunt their prey in circles, like sharks do. A wide round current marked where they circled below. Tiger Lily surfaced once, choked, and went under again.

I landed on the floating nest, skidding to a stop with one of my wings slapping against the water. It stuck, and I clung to a twig, half submerged. Touching the water, I could feel a swirl of thoughts under the surface—the muddy, half-fish thoughts of the mermaids, enraged at her betrayal, and then, clearer and more familiar, Tiger Lily. But it was like there were two of her. There was a Tiger Lily who wanted to follow Tik Tok underwater, and was unwilling to fight the mermaids off. And there was a Tiger Lily I knew from when she was a child. This Tiger Lily flailed out with both hands. She pulled her dagger from her waist and sliced out in an arc, and kicked her way up to the surface. An unearthly scream rose from under the water: one of the mermaids, mortally injured. Tiger Lily lunged at the nest, and pushed it farther, then pushed again. She saw it slam against the rock at Peter's feet as he leaned out as far as he could. Then she swam in the opposite direction. It was almost like a water ballet—the way the mermaids circled her, how they disappeared and resurfaced in the churning water, again and again as I fluttered above. Mermaid blood floated on the surface of the lagoon in buckets, iridescent and oily.

Still, I didn't believe she had a chance of making it across until she was there, scrambling up onto the muddy shore and pulling herself to safety in the dry bushes. She choked out water onto the ground, then crawled farther into the brush.

I could hear her now, her heart beating, her arms around

her legs, shivering. And I turned in time to see Peter guiding Wendy from where they'd paddled the nest to the opposite shore. I watched until they reached the water's edge, and their shadows climbed onto dry ground, disappearing into the bushes.

I don't know how a girl with lungs instead of gills survived such an attack. Even one mermaid as old and strong as Maeryn would have been more than a match for any land creature—human or otherwise. But I never saw Maeryn again after that night, and I'm quite sure Tiger Lily must have killed her.

Maybe what the villagers had said all along was true. Maybe the second Tiger Lily I heard under the water—the one who fought—was the girl who had been drowned in a vat of turkey broth but had somehow come out alive. Maybe she couldn't be drowned.

Later, Wendy would tell people on the ship that they had battled pirates. But she would never say that Tiger Lily had betrayed them, or that she had rescued them either. Because that would have meant asking a question she couldn't comprehend asking: why the native girl might have wanted her dead. It didn't fit her ideas of who was bad, and who was good, and what was a happy ending, and what wasn't.

Undetected, Tiger Lily stood, shaken and wet and cold, and made her way toward the bridge that led across the crocodile creek, and toward home.

She was just stepping onto the first creaky wooden plank when Reginald Smee caught her, finally, off her guard.

He had been waiting behind a tree, not well hidden at all. But it turned out, he hadn't needed to be. Before she knew it, his hands were around her neck. She couldn't call for help.

Even exhausted as she was, her reflexes were fast. She and Reginald slammed into one side of the bridge and then the other before she got her elbows between his arms. As she thrust them outward, breaking his hold on her neck, she also thrust him forward.

The bridge's rail splintered behind the weight. There was a moment when it seemed the rail would hold. And then a creak, and a sinking crash, and it fell away behind him as he tumbled.

The crocodiles were ready.

Tiger Lily pulled herself back from the brink as Reginald Smee fell backward and splashed into the water among the crocodiles. There was no real struggle. No scream or wet flailing about. Just a tussle among the crocs, and the snapping of many jaws, and then the dive underwater of the triumphant animal, and the water's surface was glassy and silent, as if nothing had happened at all.

There was a crunching of feet approaching in the leaves, and a second later there stood James Hook. He took in the scene all at once, his mouth open in surprise.

Tiger Lily reached for her dagger, and held it in front of

her body. They stared at each other; moments passed. "He came for me," she finally said.

Hook rubbed the back of his neck, nodding. "Yes," he said. He took one tiny step forward, looked over the place where the rail had been. "Idiot," he whispered. He hated disobedience from his men. It always made him feel empty, like once again, the world had proven that there was no one to trust. He kicked some dirt off the bridge in disgust. He let out a sigh, because he had been down this road a million times before, and it never surprised him. "Well, Peter's dead. Smee's dead. It's eat or get eaten, I guess." He was half joking, though there was no happiness in his humor. "I'm sorry," he said, and he bowed his head a little to Tiger Lily respectfully, and for a moment, you could see the good manners he'd worked so hard to achieve. "I'd better go before I'm eaten too."

He turned and limped off into the woods, rubbing at his sore back.

FORTY-THREE

Like I've said before, in a village, ideas sweep people up like tornadoes, and leave very little room for disagreement in their path. The decision was made, among the Sky Eaters, that the Englanders must go willingly, or be chased out.

The crows had taken over the village. For a full week, they invaded the Sky Eaters' homes and perched around their fires and excreted on their crops. And while the villagers knew it must be Tiger Lily's doing, they also knew that the gods were behind her. And in any case, there was a difference between Tiger Lily and the Englanders. Tiger Lily, despite her otherness, belonged to them. The Englanders did not.

It would have been shocking, to anyone from outside the village, to see how quickly they turned on the foreigners.

And the decision was made, among the Englanders, that no one would stay behind. They said it was because of the inhospitable climate, and because of obligations at home, but everyone knew it was their fear of the way the tribe looked at them now, and because of the crows.

They began to pack up their things, and the village was once again in a flurry with their comings and goings. Their imminent departure meant two things to Tiger Lily: that her tribe would go back to the old way, of watching the world around them for signs, and that Peter would be leaving the island.

She would not look at Phillip when he came to say goodbye, extending his condolences about Tik Tok without it ever seeming to cross his mind that he had played a part.

The villagers all came out to see him go, gathering on either side of the path that led out. I didn't see who threw first, but somewhere from the sidelines, an object hurtled at Phillip and struck him in the shoulder. It was one of Tik Tok's hair clips. And then came a yam. And then an ear of corn. And soon he was holding his arms around his head and rushing out under a shower of vegetables.

Tiger Lily slipped out the other side of the village, without anyone noticing.

The whole burrow had been turned upside down. What the boys were taking with them, they'd put into sacks. What they weren't, they'd left lying here and there: clay bowls, old toys, the ball that Tiger Lily had rescued from the tree. She found Peter alone in his room. He was packing things into a wooden box: his drawings; his tiny, half-finished fanciful carvings.

He turned and saw her, and then turned back to his packing. He was quiet for several moments.

"Did you hear how I rescued Wendy from drowning?" he finally asked.

"Yes," she said, agreeing to pretend.

He kept packing, as if nothing in the world was wrong.

"You got away. I'm glad."

"Yes. You're going?" she asked.

"It's funny, how fast the boys were to say yes." He stuffed a carving of a mermaid into his box. "I never expected it. I'm an idiot." He turned and met her eyes. "Yes, I'm going."

"But you loved me?" she said simply.

He stared at her for a long time. He looked much older, more serious. "I'm sorry about Tik Tok." There was no twinkle in his eyes. "Maybe I just love some of you. Maybe not enough." Tiger Lily blinked at him, and she didn't understand how anyone could only love a part. Her greedy heart didn't work that way. She turned to go.

He looked down at his fingers. "Tiger Lily, I forgive you. I really do. And you came back for me." He looked indecisive. "It's just, I think I have to leave."

"I don't understand," she said.

"It doesn't make sense. Even to me," he said. He took her

in. He seemed to hover on the edge of the choice. She felt that with one strong word, she could pull him back.

There was a long moment between them that might have gone differently. Of all the times I saw the two of them together, this is the picture that is most stamped into my soul. It's the two of them, jumbled up and broken apart into confused pieces, and not really understanding, themselves, what they were doing.

"I won't wait for you to change your mind," she finally said, her chin set stubbornly.

He bit his lip thoughtfully. "I understand." And to Tiger Lily he suddenly, inexplicably, seemed older than her, and wiser, and the thought hit her hard that it wasn't fair, because she'd suffered, and there he was, looking like he knew so much more than she ever would.

She didn't return to the village. She walked up to what was left of the stone cottage, which had the best view of the sea. And even though she'd said she wouldn't, she waited for Peter.

She couldn't tell who got on or off the ship: the people below—carrying their things aboard, packing up the last of their supplies and samples and fruits and dried meats— were only little dots. Still, she felt like she would know him even from so far away. And as far as she could tell, he didn't get on.

She was standing on the cliffs, two days after they'd

spoken, when she saw the ship pull up anchor.

Sailing ships like this one were a dying breed. Even steamships were being replaced with newer and quicker machines. They were carrying people faster, spreading them all around the globe so that there were no dark, undiscovered places anymore. Tiger Lily didn't know she was watching an extinction.

The ship drifted away from port, raised its sails, and picked up speed, taking the Englanders with it. It got smaller and smaller and farther away. Hours passed before it was only a speck disappearing into the horizon.

Tiger Lily went back into the house, from which she kept watch of the ocean. She held her arms around her stomach and stayed awake. She didn't want him to catch her sleeping.

Peter did not come that night, or the next day, and she stayed awake. She did not believe he could have really gone, because for her, to leave the person you loved was impossible.

For three days, she kept on studying the horizon, even speaking to it, as if a ship that had already disappeared could hear her. "Choose me."

And Peter did choose. But he chose something else.

FORTY-FOUR

This is my one small part. This is the one small thing I was able to change in a human life, ever.

I pulled Tiger Lily back from the brink.

After Peter left, she lay down on the mattress in the empty house, and forgot to eat.

She kept trying, in her head, to make someone right. To make Peter right or herself right or Tik Tok, because that was the only way the world could be a circle again. But they were all wrong. They had all broken each other. And this wrongness was what took her spirit away.

By the time she remembered to drink, she couldn't stand up without getting dizzy, and couldn't make it to the water. That's when she started talking to me. Her hand reached out, and she said Peter's name for me, Tinker Bell. And smiled. And told me about growing up in the village, as if I hadn't seen it myself, and talked about what it was like to be a person who everyone said was cursed by crows, and how she didn't care what they thought anyway. She told me how Pine Sap had brought the crows to scare all the Englanders away, using his bird calls to summon and keep them close, and I didn't know if it was true or false, and I don't think she did either. She said she wondered why I never went home, but that she didn't want me to.

Maybe it was the delirium that made her talk to me that way. But it kept her awake, and I think her staying awake kept her alive. I brought things I'd found for her to eat and get water from—tiny nuts and berries I knew were edible – and she let me force them between her lips. And before long, someone came looking for her, and tracked her up to the cliffs.

It was early morning when Pine Sap stood in the doorway. He sat on the bed beside her. She let herself sink against his lap. She could feel his spindly legs, smell his familiar smell.

"I could have been stronger," she said. "I wasn't enough to keep something so important."

"Tiger Lily, you're a fool," he said, and kissed her forehead. And despite his size, and the fact that a boy like him was not built to shoulder much of anything, he shouldered her weight, and carried her home.

FORTY-FIVE

S ometimes I think that maybe we are just stories. Like we may as well just be words on a page, because we're only what we've done and what we are going to do.. I know I'm only a faerie, a tiny speck in the world, but then I look at the things I've seen and done, and I become a long scrawly line of something important. And I think it's the same for Tiger Lily and Peter and even Tik Tok and for my father and for Belladonna, the faerie he ran away with, and for Maeryn and maybe every fish in the sea.

I know that there are different kinds of stories with different kinds of endings. But I can't say that, for Tiger Lily, it worked that way, with any kind of ending I could pin down. And there were still things I didn't expect.

The first was that Tiger Lily kept Tik Tok's promise. She

married Giant in a ceremony in the square.

It was like every other wedding that had happened in the village, though a shaman from another village had to come to perform the ceremony. There was dancing and binding and promising. She wore the dress Tik Tok had made her, and Giant looked sullen and ravenous at the same time. But he did not touch her that night. It was as though the arrival of the crows had finally put the fear into him that all the others had felt long ago.

Another thing I didn't expect was that within two weeks of his wedding night, Giant was dead.

He had been taking a nap alone in his house, but he never woke up. People ascribed it to Tiger Lily's curse. But they also whispered that he had gotten what he deserved. Aunt Sticky Feet whispered something different. She said she'd seen Moon Eye walking out of his house that afternoon, with an old clay jar of Tik Tok's. But Aunt Sticky Feet was known to be an alarmist. And even I never knew for sure.

Things were quiet for a long time. We passed the hours the way we always had, and one day leaked into another, and the quiet lasted and lasted. It was fifty years before another ship docked near Neverland's shores. But what is fifty years when you're not growing any older?

It was by this time that even the remotest corners of the globe were no longer remote. The mermaids had retreated into the deepest parts of the ocean, lucky to be able to go somewhere they would never be found. The faeries hid, too, in the island's thickest swamps, and far away from the shore. The tribe didn't have to. The visitors never came near them.

Still, I noticed a curious sight one morning when I was down on the beach, looking for pieces of the best sand to go in my hair: Tiger Lily in a canoe, paddling out to talk to them. She was still curious. Phillip had not killed her restlessness to know. And they offered for her to go with them if she was so curious. There would be ships coming back this direction in a year or so.

Pine Sap said once that he would rather die than see Tiger Lily tamed. I guess Tiger Lily felt the same about Peter, because she stayed behind. And that is how I, Tink, went to England, instead of her. Because as always, my curiosity outweighed my fear.

I arrived in London in early spring—took up residence in a bush by the docks, where I could keep an eye on the lizards and flies, which were small and unintimidating. I was dazzled and awed by the girls, the dresses, the electric lights, and the buildings made of stone. I also immediately longed for home, the woods, the river, even my swamp. I wanted to leave London almost as soon as I arrived.

As the days passed, I put off seeing Peter. I found other things to do. Weeks trickled by, and still, I steered clear of the neighborhood Wendy had talked about, which I found on maps but did not visit.

It was only toward the end of my stay, during a winter of a kind of coldness I could never have imagined, and when I knew one of the rare ships that sailed close to Neverland was slated to depart in two days, that I found my way to Finsbury Circus, and the big yellow house. I was both relieved and unnerved to find that it still stood, exactly as Wendy had described it.

That afternoon, I had seen snow for the first time. It muffled everything, and made it feel so silent and gave me a quiet feeling, just a peacefulness and a waiting for new things to grow. It was cold, and my wings moved stiffly. My breath puffed out around me, but no one in London paid attention to insects. Up on the second floor, there was a balcony. I flew up unnoticed, and looked in the window.

There was no one home. But peering through the glass, I couldn't imagine anywhere more comfortable and safe, or more like everything Peter had always said he didn't want. It was a room full of books, but unmistakably, it had Peter's stamp on it. His carvings sat on various shelves, miraculously complete. An old handmade bow sat in the corner. A plant sat on the windowsill—grown from a cutting I recognized. It was a big-leafed, wild-looking plant that grew all over Neverland. It crept up the corner near the glass, and seemed to have a life of its own, branching out in all crooked directions. I wondered what had prompted Peter to keep it. As if he could keep the wilderness in a pot.

But even now, without him there, it was impossible to think of him in the comfortable room, growing older and breathing indoor air. Fifty years later, and I still didn't understand him.

A door opened to the left, and my breath caught, because in he came. I was frozen still, peering in, unable to move, and sure he wouldn't see me, but his eyes went to me immediately. A huge smile spread across his face and he walked to the window, and pulled it open, the warm air spilling out on me as I'm sure the cold air spilled in. Only, it wasn't Peter. The nose was different. The teeth were bigger. There was no savage about the eyes. I realized my mistake.

He opened the window. "You can't be real," he said. He must have been twenty or more years old. I flapped my wings, trying to acknowledge him. He appeared utterly flustered, his cheeks bright red, puffing in amazement. He reached for me, but I zipped backward.

"Sarah, come look!" he yelled over his shoulder. He turned to me. "Are you looking for my father?" he asked, half joking.

He seemed to be speaking rhetorically, and must have considered me a dumb creature. He reached out and petted the top of my head, with Peter's gentle touch. "He's walking in the park, little one. Come in from the cold. You're a treasure!" He reached out again to catch me, but I finally found my wits and flew back and away, and swooped down above the street. I was gone before he could employ a more effective tool to capture me. The Englanders, I knew, loved

286

to study things to death.

On my way toward the house earlier, I'd flown past the park—a big oval, powdered pure white, below me. I found Peter there. He was walking in a direction away from the house, and I flew in behind him. I would have known his thin chicken-wing shoulders anywhere. I knew his animal gait, even when he moved slowly.

I'd never seen Peter in a coat. From the back, he was gray-haired. I flew closer, so that I could see the pores of skin on his neck, my tiny heart in my throat, and suddenly my courage left me. It turned out that my curiosity did not outweigh my courage after all. Sometimes love means not being able to bear seeing the one you love the way they are, when they're not what you hoped for them. I turned and went back to the docks, and waited the two days for my ship to leave. It was the last I would ever see of Peter.

By the time I got home, a year had passed. And much had changed.

The most surprising thing, to me, was that Tiger Lily and Pine Sap were to be married.

She talked to me now. After the stone house, she hadn't stopped. She told me they had just been walking into the river one day, getting ready for their usual swim, when she knew. She said she thought there were different ways of loving some-one, and there were some she used to think were the most important, and now she had changed her mind.

287

For weeks, I saw it as a tragic turn of events. But when I tried to see him through Tiger Lily's eyes, I began to see it differently. She laughed with him, more often than she had laughed with Peter. Her heart beat strong and steady around him, as if he gave it strength. I could hear that she loved every piece of his crooked face, without an ounce of fear.

Some words meant something different to Tiger Lily than they ever had before; some sentences waited years to grow full in her mind. Many people in the village wanted her to be more of a girl, and Peter had wanted her to be large and brave but a little less large and brave than him. But Pine Sap was sure enough to want her to be exactly who she was. And though there were many people who loved Tiger Lily in her tribe, and many people Tiger Lily loved, that was what she was left with. There were three people who loved her exactly as she was. Tik Tok. Pine Sap. And me.

Their marriage surprises me all the time, because it's always changing. It looks nothing like the love Tiger Lily had with Peter, but it is as big in its own way. They go swimming in the reeds together, and she holds on to Pine Sap's neck and wraps her legs around him and he swims like a dolphin. In the water, he can carry her. They sit in front of their home that Pine Sap built and he calls the birds to her fingers and she laughs that easy laugh. Sometimes she treks in the woods without him for days. But at home Pine Sap talks about poems and the countless things he thinks about, and Tiger Lily feels as though his mind is a forest, too, and that she is discovering a new place.

Their daughters are hungry, joyful little souls, but only one of them is half feral like her mother. The other is as girlish as any girl ever born. Moon Eye, who surprised everyone by living as long as anyone, also surprised them by marrying a Bog Dweller she met at a gathering of the shamans, after she took on Tik Tok's role as medicine woman.

I don't know when Tiger Lily stopped growing older; I can't pinpoint the moment. But I do know I never saw her visibly age beyond the days when she was with Peter. I like to think her growing stopped the day they were on the plateau, watching the horses. Sometimes I can almost convince myself that on the ridge that night, I actually heard her bones grinding to a halt, her skin pause, because that simple day was the most important thing that would ever happen to her. Just an afternoon, when nothing amazing occurred, except that she felt completely happy and completely at home. But truthfully, even I couldn't have heard these things.

Now there are days when she is content, and days when she's restless. But there is never a day when she doesn't see Peter everywhere. Things hurt, and don't hurt, and hurt again. Eighty years later, and she can still feel surprised that he's gone. And then so much of the time, she's glad. But just as she looks for Tik Tok in everything around her, she looks for Peter in the woods, out gathering, in the lagoon, in the burrow that is now abandoned. She goes up on the cliffs from time to time and stands there for hours, continuing her long good-bye. It's not for lack of loyalty to her husband. It is just that she was fifteen once for the first time, and Peter walked across her heart, and left his footprints there.

For my own part, I must admit I spend more and more time thinking that I should go home. I keep wondering if it's time to be back with my own family, and to be somewhere that feels like I belong there, even if it isn't perfect. And I keep putting it off. I am always saying, when the moon has set thirty more times, that is when I'll go back to the swamp. But I keep on staying.

There is one more thing I'll give you. One more piece of their story. And Tiger Lily didn't tell it to me. I discovered it myself.

I said I never saw Peter again. But I did hear of him, or from him in a way, one night years later, while chasing a moth that had somehow managed to wedge itself into the folds under Tiger Lily's bedroll. That was when I found the last words I'd ever get from Peter. The envelope was covered in stamps, and wrinkled, warped from water, crinkly and wavy like the sea that countless ships had carried it across. The letter had been folded and unfolded so many times that it had gotten soft as velvet. She had managed to keep it a secret even from me, who listened to her head on a daily basis.

It wasn't surprising that he had learned to write. But here is some of what it said:

Did you know I always thought you were braver than me?
Did you ever guess that that was why I was so afraid? It
wasn't that I only loved some of you. But I wondered if you
could ever love more than some of me.

I knew I'd miss you. But the surprising thing is, you
never leave me. I never forget a thing. Every kind of love, it
seems, is the only one. It doesn't happen twice. And I never
expected that you could have a broken heart and love with it
too, so much that it doesn't seem broken at all. I know young
people look at me and think my youth seems so far away.
But it's all around me, and you're all around me. Tiger
Lily, do you think magic exists if it can be explained? I can
explain why I loved you, I can explain the theory of evolution
that tells me why mermaids live in Neverland and nowhere
else. But it still feels magic.

The lost boys all stood at our wedding. Does it seem odd
to you that they could have stood at a wedding that wasn't
yours and mine? It does to me. And I'm sorry for it, and for a
lot, and I also wouldn't change it.

It is so quiet here. Even with all the trains and the streets
and the people. It's nothing like the jungle. The boys have
grown. Everything has grown. Do you think you will ever
grow? I hope not. I like to think that even if I change and
fade away, some other people won't.

I like to think that one day after I die, at least one
small particle of me—of all the particles that will spread
everywhere—will float all the way to Neverland, and be part

*of a flower or something like that, like that poet said, the one
that your Tik Tok loved. I like to think that nothing's final,
and that everyone gets to be together even when it looks like
they don't, that it all works out even when all the evidence
seems to say something else, that you and I are always
young in the woods, and that I'll see you sometime again,
even if it's not with any kind of eyes I know of or understand.
I wouldn't be surprised if that is the way things go after all—
that all things end happy. Even for you and Tik Tok. And for
you and me.*

Always,

Your Peter

*P.S. Please give my love to Tink. She was always such a
funny little bug.*

ACKNOWLEDGMENTS

Thank you to Sarah Landis, Kari Sutherland, and Zareen Jaffrey for being so elegantly intelligent as they nurtured this book, to Melinda Weigel for giving it her careful attention, and to all the folks at Harper for always treating me so nicely. Thank you to Tara and Misha, who were early to encourage me to keep thinking about Tiger Lily and Peter; Rosemary Stimola for always putting the important things first; Liesa and James, Ben Cawood, and Maria Bejarano for all sorts of grounding and encouragement; my family for their limitless enthusiasm; and Mark for his faith in me.